Broken

©2019 Lakisha Johnson

Published by Lakisha Johnson | Twins Write 2 Publishing

Edition License Notes

This book is a work of fiction, made up by the author. If there is any place, storyline or name comparable to anything; it is purely coincidental. This paperback book is written and licensed for your personal enjoyment only and should not be re-sold. If you would like to share this book with another person, please purchase an additional copy for each recipient. Thank you for respecting the hard work of this author.

Dedication

This book is dedicated to all the men who had or has a hand in raising me.

My grandfather, Mr. Robert Rucker, Sr. (Rest in Peace)

My Daddy-in-love, Mr. Willie Johnson, Sr.

My Step-dad, Isaac Stovall

My uncles; Johnny (RIP), George, Larry, LB, Buddy, David and Tommy Rucker.

These men have shaped my life, in some way and I love each of them, unconditionally.

My Gratefulness

I start every word of thanks the same because it is to God whom I owe everything. If it wasn't for the gifts, He so graciously etched within me, I wouldn't be able to do what I love. To write and encourage.

As always, I am grateful to my family and friends who gives, unwavering support.

I am also grateful to every one of you, who support me through every book published. I would not be the author I am without readers like you. It is because of you purchasing, reading, reviewing and recommending that pushes me to be greater with each release. Thank you from the bottom of my heart!

Now, let's get to flipping!

Broken

"Now we see things imperfectly, like puzzling reflections in a mirror, but then we will see everything with perfect clarity. All that I know, now, is partial and incomplete, but then I will know everything completely, just as God now knows me completely. Three things will last forever--faith, hope, and love-- and the greatest of these is love."

– 1 Corinthians 13:12-13 NLT

Jacque

"Gwen, did you hear me? Hello! Earth to Gwen!"

She snatches the headphones, from her ears, when her eyes open to see me snapping my fingers in her face.

"Jacque, you scared me," she says putting her hand on her chest. "I didn't realize you were home. What did you say?"

"Nothing," I reply plopping down on the bed to remove my shoes.

"I'm sorry, I was reading and listening to this new song we're learning for women's day."

I look back at her and roll my eyes.

"Why are you rolling your eyes? What's wrong with you?"

"Nothing Gwen and I'm not in the mood to argue," I state, agitated.

"Who's arguing? You said something I didn't hear and I asked you to repeat it."

"For what? It's not like you're going to listen. You always got your face in a book or handling church business. You do realize you have a whole husband, right? Unless there's something you have to tell me."

"Jacque, please don't start this tonight," she tells me while turning off the music, closing the book and removing her glasses.

"Start what Gwen? A conversation with my wife. Hell, I'm just being honest. You're either reading or most of the time, you're down at High Point. I'm starting to think you're screwing the pastor."

She chuckles. "First off, my pastor is a woman. You'd know that if you were to come to worship with me. Secondly, how would you know what I'm doing or where I am, when you're rarely here? Mayyybeeee," she drags out, "if my husband would stop working late, every night of the week, he'd get to see my face and my body."

I jump up and throw my shoes next to the dresser. "I have to work late to pay for this five thousand square foot house, that 2019 Mercedes you just got and all the clothes and shoes filling three closets."

I stop when I see her lip syncing, word for word, what I'm saying.

"Don't mock me Gwen."

"Mane, I'm not mocking you but aren't you tired of giving that same speech because I'm tired of hearing it? Look, you are not the only one working yet I still find time to cook meals you don't eat and clean the house, YOU wanted, but hardly see. Furthermore, I only have two closets."

She stands up and starts grabbing her phone and book.

"Where are you going?"

"To sleep in the other room before one of us say something we can't take back."

"Gwen wait," I say grabbing her arm. "I'm sorry."

She snatches away. "Don't touch me."

"I'm trying to apologize."

"What's the point when we'll have this same argument tomorrow?"

"That's not true."

"Yes, it is and you know it. You are barely here and when you do show up, all you want to do is argue. Hell, you'd think you were a nagging wife," she sighs. "I'm tired and if you aren't happy, say it so we can get off this merry-go-round because I'm forty-years-old, too old for games and not in the business of keeping someone who doesn't want to be kept."

I grab her hand. "I am where I want to be but—"

"But what?" She questions, cocking her head to the side. "But what Jacque?"

"Nothing."

"No, finish the sentence. But what? Are you cheating on me?"

"No! Why is that the first thing you think of? Can't I be tired too? DAMN!"

"You need to lower your voice," she orders stepping back from me, "because I'm not yelling at you."

"I'm sorry."

"Dude, what's really going on because you haven't been the same lately."

I take a deep breath. "Babe, I'm not cheating on you. I'm just stressed with all the changes at the office and my new boss but it's no excuse to take out my frustration on you. Will you forgive me?"

She stares at me.

"Gwen, I promise that's all it is."

"If you say so but let me remind you of the promise you made—"

"Not to break your heart," I finish. "I won't."

"You better not because then I'll be on an episode of Snapped with my blinged-out orange jumpsuit, from Bertha on the block while they continually show me smiling on my mugshot."

I shake my head as I watch her walk into the bathroom before I go into the closet and undress. When I'm done, I stop at the door of the closet when I see her bending over the bed in this short nightgown.

"Um, Mrs. London, what are you wearing?"

"Um, Mr. London, this is called a nightgown."

I walk up behind her.

"No," she tells me. "We both know sex isn't going to fix whatever is happening between us."

She gets into bed and covers up.

"Gwen, I know I haven't been the best husband lately and although I've apologized, a lot, I really am sorry."

"An apology means nothing without the actions. The Bible says—"

"Here we go with this Bible crap," I gripe, flinging my arm. "Just tell me what you want me to do and I'll do it."

"That's part of the problem. Jacque, you're the head of our household yet you've stopped allowing God to be your head. When that happens, the enemy is bound to come in. Look, I'm not asking you to perform miracles. All I want are the following things. Number one, you need to listen. Numbers two through five; be the husband you vowed to be, have dinner with your wife sometimes, be home for me to lay in your arms while we discuss our day and God knows we need a vacation."

"I hear you," he says.

"But are you listening?"

"Yes, and to show you, I am going to plan a weekend getaway, for us and we'll leave tomorrow."

She laughs, "Is that all you heard?"

"No, but can I start somewhere?"

"Fine but you know as well as I do, you'll end up canceling."

"Not this time. I have a few meetings that are too late to reschedule but once I'm done, we can hit the road."

She rolls her eyes.

"I promise. Tell you what, to show you, I'll pack my bag tonight and leave it by the door. Then, tomorrow, you can drop me off and when you pick me up, we can get out of here."

"Where are we going?"

"I don't know yet but I'll take care of it. You just make sure to pack a bikini."

"If you lie to me this time—"

"You'll see." I say falling on top of her.

Gwen

He begins kissing me.

"I love you Gwen and I am going to fix this."

"You better because we've been in this thang too long, to let it end like this."

"I know and I will make it up to you, starting right now."

He continues to kiss all over my face before sitting up to remove my night gown.

"Wait Jacque, stop. You need to get a condom."

"I don't want to use one, not tonight," he replies, placing his hand between my legs.

"You know I am out of birth control pills."

"Good, maybe we can go half on a baby."

"Boy, we ain't making no baby when we are barely making it. Get a condom or get on your side of the bed."

He grunts before reaching over to the nightstand, on his side of the bed where he snatches the drawer open, almost falling. I shake my head. Taking out the box, he rolls over on his back and quickly covers his manhood.

Grabbing my leg, he pulls me to him. He starts to kiss on my neck while entering me and I moan my pleasure. He moves slowly, at first and it feels so good. I close my eyes but they don't stay closed because he stops and flips me over. Before I can react, he puts his hand on the back of my head and pushes me into the bed.

"Jacque," I call out but he doesn't stop. Instead he starts pounding like a man fresh off a ten-year prison sentence.

"Slow down. Ah, Jacque, slow down. JACQUE!"

He abruptly stops so I push him off and jump up, pulling the fallen head wrap from over my eyes.

"What the hell was that?" I demand to know. "You were hurting me."

"I-uh—"

"You can't speak now? You almost broke my damn neck and all you can say is I-uh. Negro, you need to get your shit together and quick because you better not ever try that again." I walk into the bathroom and slam the door.

The next morning, I roll over and reach for Jacque.

"Jacque?"

When I look at the clock on the nightstand, I realize it's after eight and he's already gone. I grab my phone and see a text from him.

JACQUE: GM Babe! I had to come in earlier and didn't want to disturb you. I'll be home by six and we can hit the road.

I didn't even bother to respond because I knew better.

A couple of hours later, I walk into London Page, the real estate company I own with my older sister, Gloria.

"Hey, I didn't think you were coming in."

"I wasn't but I wanted to get the inspection finalized on the Waldorf project."

"You know I can handle that. Besides, shouldn't you be at home packing for your weekend getaway?"

"Girl, we both know Jacque is going to cancel."

"Maybe he won't this time," she says.

"Yea, we'll see."

I grab the files, needed and head over to the building site for the home being built for my clients, Mr. and Mrs. Cliff Waldorf. I spend more time than I'd planned, dealing with last minute items that had to be completed. Rushing to get in the car, it's after four so I text Jacque.

ME: Hey! I haven't heard from you today. Are we still on?

JACQUE: Hey babe, I've been swamped but yes. I'll be out of here by six SHARP!

ME: If you stand me up, don't bother coming home.

JACQUE: I won't, I promise.

I place my bag by the door, next to Jacque's bag that was already packed. Looking at my watch, I still have an hour before he's supposed to be home.

"Good timing Gwen, you might be able to finish this episode of My 600LB Life," I say to myself, grabbing the remote and getting comfortable on the couch.

"Gwen, babe."

"Hmm, what?" I open my eyes and see Jacque, kneeling next to the couch.

"Babe, I'm so sorry. I got caught up in a meeting and time got away from me."

I look at my watch.

"Really? That's the best you could come up with? Jacque, it's after ten and you reek of alcohol and smoke."

"I know but that's because the owner wanted to take everybody out to celebrate me landing the biggest account ever."

"Congratulations but I hope those same men, you're allowing to keep you away from your wife, can handle my responsibilities when I'm gone." I get up from the couch.

"Gwen, wait."

"No, you wait. I am fed up with your empty promises and blatant lies. You were the one who said you were going to plan for us to leave tonight, not me. However, the real issue is, I already knew you were going to back out yet I still allowed you to hurt my feelings."

"You were the one who said we needed a vacation," he replies, casually.

"WE DO!" I take a deep breath. "I'm tired of this, tired of the arguing and unresolved issues Jacque."

"What are you saying?"

"I'm saying, if you want out, take it and I can promise, I will not fight you." I walk into the bedroom and slam the door, locking it.

Jacque

I get up early Saturday morning to cook breakfast, to make up for last night. When I hear the bedroom door open, I have a red rose waiting for Gwen but when she turns the corner, fully dressed, I take a step back.

"Hey, where are you going?"

"Out," she states.

"Babe, wait."

"What Jacque, I'm running late."

"I fixed breakfast and thought we could talk," I say handing her the rose.

She snatches it and throws it back at me. "Dude, if you think a rose and some breakfast is going to make up for everything, you're mistaken. I'm going to say this again for the fourth or fifth time, in two days, I AM TIRED."

"I heard you and I'm sorry. I never want to make you feel like it's time to give up on our marriage. I love you Gwendolyn London and I'll do whatever it takes to make you see that."

"Yea and like Sunshine Anderson sings, I've heard it all before. Show me."

She grabs a piece of bacon and turn to head out the door but I grab her hand.

"Jacque, let me go because I don't have time to keep rehashing the same tired conversation with no actions."

I hold up two plane tickets.

"What's that supposed to prove? They are probably for 2020."

"Look at them," I offer.

She yanks them from my hand. "Today?"

"Yes, today and I'm glad you're already dressed and your bag is packed."

"Don't play with me Jacque. Is this for real? Hawaii? This is a long and expensive flight just to come back in two days."

"We're not coming back in two days."

"Oh my God, we're going for an entire week?" She squeals after looking at the tickets again.

I take her hand. "Gwen, I love you and I know I haven't been showing it lately but I do and I want our marriage."

"I love you too but I don't want you to think that it's only about a vacation. I want to see more of you, at home. I get that your job is important, so is mine but I make time for what's important and that's you."

"I know and I'm going to do better," I reply kissing her.

"Okay, now move because I need to pack."

"I thought you were already packed."

"Boy, I knew you were lying about yesterday and that's why there's nothing in that bag but paper," I laugh.

"Hold up, didn't you have somewhere to be this morning?"

"Nope, I was lying."

"Then where were you going?"

"To Target."

I laugh as she grabs her bag, sitting next to the door and runs to the bedroom.

***

After a long day of traveling, we finally make it to Honolulu. We get to our resort and once we're done checking in, we are too tired to do anything else. Gwen orders some food and we stay in. The next morning, we get up early for our couple's massage, I'd reserved ahead of time.

I allow her to walk in while I take a call from work.

"Welcome to Waikiki Resort & Spa. Can I have your name, please?"

"Gwen London."

"Mrs. London, do you have a reservation?"

"It's probably under Jacque London. J-A-C-Q-U-E."

"No, I'm sorry but I, oh wait, I have Mr. London under another reservation and—no worries, I have it taken care of."

"What do you mean another reservation? With who?" I question.

"Graft Enterprises and a —"

"That should have been changed," Jacque interjects.

"It has been Mr. London. You and your wife can follow me."

I can see Gwen looking at me, out the corner of her eye but I keep walking.

Two hours later, we're leaving the spa.

"Mr. London, you are pulling out all the stops," Gwen smiles grabbing my hand.

"Did you enjoy it?"

"Yes, and this entire resort is amazing. How did you find it?"

"A co-worker suggested it."

"Is that why the massages were under the company's name?"

"Yes, I had Sasha book them."

She nods without saying anything else.

We spend the next six days enjoying Hawaii and each other. I can't remember the last time we've had time away and fun, together. An added bonus, it felt good to see Gwen smile again.

***

"Ladies and gentleman, welcome to Memphis, TN where it is currently 7:48PM on June 17, 2018 and the temperature is a hot, 82 degrees. For your safety and comfort, please remain seated with your seat belt fastened until the Captain turns off the fasten seat belt sign—"

"Jacque, thank you for doing this."

"Anything for you baby. I love you with all of me."

"I love you too."

Gwen

It's been about two months since Jacque and I went on vacation. Things between us have been going great. He's been at home more and has put forth an effort to make our marriage work. We even have plans to spend the New Year holiday in the mountains of Gatlinburg, TN.

Tonight, he's working late and I decide to bring him dinner before I head home. I sent him a text, earlier, but he hasn't responded so when I pull up to the office building, I call his desk but he doesn't answer it either. I send another text, no reply. After waiting a few more minutes, I turn the car off and walk to the door where security buzzes me in.

"Mrs. London, I haven't seen you in forever. How have you been?" Charlene in security asks, getting up to give me a hug.

"I am good Charlene. How is the new baby? Did Jacque give you the gift I sent?"

"She is perfect and yes, it was very beautiful. I gave him a thank you card with some pictures."

"We both know that card is probably still in his briefcase."

She laughs. "Do you want me to let him know you're here?"

"Please."

She buzzes his office but she doesn't get an answer either. "Hmm, I know he's here."

"Is it okay if I go on up? I'm just dropping off some dinner."

"Sure. Let me give you a badge."

I take the sticker from her. "Thanks, and it was good seeing you Charlene."

"You too."

I get on the elevator and press the 11th floor. When the door finally opens, I get off to a mostly dark floor. Not surprising seeing most people, besides my husband, leave at five and it's now almost seven.

I turn the corner and head to his office. The door is open but he isn't here. I put my keys and container on the table before walking over to see his phone and keys still on the desk. I press the home button and see my missed calls and texts.

I turn to walk away when I notice the messenger box open on his computer. The last message is from his boss, M. Anton, summoning him to his office.

"An hour ago," I say out loud.

I pause but then I shake it off before sitting in his chair with my feet on the desk. I pull my phone from my pocket and begin to scroll through Facebook while I wait. I get caught up in the foolishness of social media and before I realize it, it has been twenty minutes. I get up and walk out of his office.

Jacque was recently promoted so I didn't know exactly which office his new boss has but I knew the name. I follow the signs to the hall of offices for senior level management. Turning the corner, I stop to read the names on the outside door plates but I notice there is only one office with the light on. I walk to the door to knock but it isn't closed all the way.

I push it open a little but I don't hear anything. I stick my head in and no one is sitting at the desk. I was about to turn around but I got a strange feeling so I decide to go inside. I open the door, wider and walk in. Looking to my right, I stop in my tracks.

My hand flies to my mouth and tears sting my eyes. Standing there to get over the shock, I pull my phone out and snap a few pictures of the scene before me. My husband and, who I assumed is his boss, are naked and asleep in each other's arms on the couch.

I crack my neck, slide my phone into my back pocket and wipe my tears. I look around the office and see a golf club, in one corner. I grab it and begin destroying the office. At the sound of glass breaking, they both jump up.

"What the—" The boss yells.

"Gwen! Oh my God!"

"Oh, you do remember God?" I ask swinging the club.

"Stop," Jacque screams running over to me.

I swing the club in his direction, hitting his hand.

"Aw!"

"So, this is what we're doing now? Sleeping around?" I yell before wiping all the glass off the wet bar. "I specifically asked you, a few months ago, if you were cheating and you said no."

Tears were streaming down my face as I move to the desk.

"Baby, please, I can explain."

"You can explain?" I repeat, swinging the club. "Let me guess, it's not what it looks like? Well, you're a got-damn lie because it looks like you fell asleep after screwing your boss. Am I wrong?"

I hit the laptop.

"Yeah, I mean no, I mean—baby, please wait."

"Wait? Are you serious? You're standing in front of me, naked with the smell of sex all over you and you want me to wait? Negro, kill yourself or better yet, come closer and I'll take care of it."

"Jacque, you need to get control of your wife." The boss interjects, with wide eyes. "She's destroying my office."

"Beloved, this isn't the only thing I plan on destroying. Wait until it becomes known my husband is sleeping with his boss, at the office. How do you think this picture," I ask unlocking my phone and turning it around, "will look in the company's newsletter?"

"Gwen, please, you don't have to do this?" Jacque whines.

"Do what? Show the world my husband is sleeping around with random people?"

"I am a lot of things but random isn't one." The boss, matter-of-factly adds. "My name is Mark," he extends his hand towards me. "Mark Anton."

Jacque

"I suggest you take that nasty hand and cover that little thing up, Mark Anton." Gwen says pointing to Mark's privates with the golf club.

"Baby, ain't nothing little about this monster," he says grabbing himself and laughing. "You're just jealous your husband wants me."

"Mark, stop!" I plea, pulling him away from her.

She laughs. "Girl, if you think I'm jealous of somebody with a small pink penis, you're mistaken. You can have Jacque and all his glory. As a matter of fact, what time are y'all coming to get his stuff out of my house?"

"What?" Mark asks wiping the smile off his face. "What do you mean?"

"Oh, Mr. Smart Mouth, is that going to cramp your style? Well, I dare not stand in the way of true love. So, what time will you all be at MY house to get your boyfriend's belongings? Or are you the boy and he, the girl?"

Mark and I look at each other.

"Baby, can we talk?" I request stepping in between her and Mark.

"No sir. All we have to talk about is what time you and your girlfriend will be there to collect your belongings."

"Babe, please let's talk about this," I beg.

"Oh, now you want to talk? You should have wanted to talk before you put your funky penis in me, over and over, knowing you've been ramming your boss in the butt."

"Jacque, what is she talking about? You said you weren't sleeping with her." Mark questions with confusion all over his face.

"What difference does it make? You're sleeping with your wife!" I yell at Mark.

"No, don't try to turn this on me because you know my relationship is only an agreement and I'm not sleeping with her."

I smash the awards, he had sitting on a shelf, to get their attention. They both jump.

"Isn't this cute, a lover's spat? I could stand here and watch you two lovebirds argue but nah, I'd rather not. However, you can shoot me a text, Jacque, when you're on your way to get your shit out of my house." She turns to walk out, wiping sweat from her forehead.

I rush to get dressed and Mark grabs my arm.

"Where are you going?"

I turn around and push him against the wall, with my forearm pressed at his throat. "I'm going to get my wife and if you know what's best for you, you wouldn't stop me."

I release him and run out of his office, with my shirt in my hand. Getting to the door of my office, I see her at my computer with the golf club in the air.

"Gwen, please don't, I'm sorry."

"You're sorry, yeah you truly are," she replies swinging at the computer. "All I've ever asked of you was to not break my heart." She knocks the pictures, of us, off the desk. "That's all. You know my past and you promised. YOU PROMISED ME!"

"I didn't mean for you to find out like this."

"Oh, so you had plans to tell me that you're gay but in twelve years, you just never got around to it? Cool."

"I messed up and you have every right to be mad."

"Thanks for the permission." She says clearing the wet bar, spilling liquor and water everywhere. She stops, breathing hard and walking towards me with the club over her shoulder. "Tell me something Jacque, that night when you came home and I made the comment about the men here being able to handle my wifely duties; why didn't you say something then?"

"I didn't know how."

"Then what was the point of taking me on vacation? Was it just to appease me and shut me up?"

I drop my head.

"Wow!"

She breaks the pictures hanging on the wall.

"I never intended to break your heart Gwen. You've got to believe me."

"I don't have to do anything Jacque. You should have been honest with me and because you couldn't, I'm done."

"Look," I say walking closer to her. "I know I've made a mess of things and broken the trust between us but can you please not tell anyone about this? Not until we figure this out?"

She laughs.

"Gwen—"

She holds her hand up while continuing to laugh.

"Oh, oh my God." She laughs, trying to catch her breath.

"Gwen, this is serious."

She instantly stops laughing, causing me to take a step back.

"Gwen, this is serious," she mocks. "Go to hell! I ought to bash your freaking head in for asking a stupid question like that. There's nothing to figure out. You and I, done!" She drops the club and walks pass me.

"Gwen please! Mark and I could lose out jobs." I blurt.

"Nig-guh!" She sounds out, slowly turning to face me. "You clearly must be drunk in love if you think I give a damn about you and your girlfriend's financial issues for the future. However, I'll do you this favor."

"So, you're not going to say anything?"

"Nope."

I release the breath I was holding. "Thank you."

"No thanks needed boo. I never had plans to tell anybody because pictures are worth a thousand words." She turns, grabs her keys from the table and walks out while waving her phone in the air, "but good luck to y'all."

I walk over to the table; the only place she didn't destroy and see a small box laying on top of the to-go container. I open it and my legs get weak as the positive pregnancy test drops from my hand.

Gwen

Getting off the elevator, I run into Charlene.

"Mrs. London, are you okay? Did you find your husband?"

"I sure did Charlene." I reply, smoothing my hair back into place. "He was asleep in his boss's arms," I answer nonchalantly.

"He—I'm sorry, he what?"

"And his boss is a man. How's that for breakroom gossip?"

I continue out the building and to my car. I get in and throw my keys and phone on the seat. Pressing the start button, I get ready to put the car in reverse when I see Jacque running out the building with his dress shirt still hanging open.

"Gwen! Please wait!"

I throw a finger sign and pull off.

Getting home, I go straight for my laptop to load the pictures to my iCloud account. After saving everything, I head into the closet to get my secret stash of weed but seeing Jacque's clothes sets me off. I begin snatching them from the hangers.

"How could you? How could you do this to me?" I scream and cry. "You promised you wouldn't do this to me."

When I'm done, I drag myself out of the closet and sit on the side of the bed. My legs are shaking and my skin is hot from the rage coursing through me. I think about calling Gloria but I wasn't ready to say, my husband is gay, to anybody yet.

"Forget this!"

Forty-five minutes, I am standing in front of the floor length mirror in the guest room. After a shower and oiling my body, I slipped into some fishnet stockings, black shorts and a black and white tunic shirt that is long in the back. Zipping up my black booties, I apply some lip gloss before taking a picture in the mirror.

I open Instagram and post the picture with a caption, 'can't beat them, you may as well join them.'"

Getting to the car, I start it and let the garage up. I don't get the car in reverse before I get a text from my sister, Gloria.

HER: Uh, where are you going and who are you joining?

I don't reply because I don't need her talking me out of whatever I'm about to get into.

I decide to visit BB Kings, on Beale St. downtown.

"How many?" The girl ask over the live band.

"One."

"It's going to be about thirty minutes before I can get you a table."

"I'll wait."

I go over to the bar and order a shot of Patron along with a Memphis Blues Margarita. A young lady motions for me to take the seat next to her.

"Thanks," I say taking the stool.

"No problem, my best friend had to leave. I'm Angel."

"Gwen."

The bartender sits my drinks in front of me and I quickly pick the shot up and decide against it.

"Here Angel, drinks on me tonight."

"Are you sure? Are you a recovering addict or something?" She questions.

"Or something," I reply ordering a Sprite.

Two hours and a lot of dancing later, I am grinding against some lady's son who has been keeping me company.

"Would you like to get out of here?" He asks into my ear.

"Sure, where to?"

"My house or yours."

"Mine, let's go." I turn and walk off, without looking back.

"Hey, wait." I hear him yell when I get to the front door. "You didn't give me your address."

"I didn't plan on it but you can follow me there."

"Cool, let me grab my jacket and I'll meet you in the parking lot."

Pulling into the driveway, I get out of the car and wait until dude parks and walks to where I am before letting the garage down.

He begins to kiss me.

"Hold on, let me turn off this alarm."

He is standing behind me, kissing on my neck but I stop when I notice the alarm was set to stay instead of away.

"That's odd."

"What is?" He asks, still kissing me.

"Nothing," I reply, punching in the code.

Turning back to him, he presses me against the wall and when he licks my ear, I laugh.

"GWEN!"

We both jump at the sound of Jacque's voice.

"Don't stop," I say to dude, "ignore him."

"Who is he, your roommate?"

"My husband."

"Wait, lady, you never said you were married," he says stepping back from me.

"You never asked."

"Man, I don't know you and you don't know me." Jacque says pulling him away from me. "To keep it that way, I suggest you get the hell out of my house."

"Sir, I apologize and don't want any problems." He walks out and I hear the garage go up.

"So, you can get your rocks off but I can't?" I sigh. "I hope you're here to get your stuff and where's your truck?"

"Is that all you're going to say after you were about to sleep with another man in our house?"

"Yep," I answer walking pass him.

He grabs my arm. "Have you been drinking?"

"Get your hands off me!" I snatch away from him. "What I do is none of your got-damn business anymore. You lost that privilege when you started ramming your boss in the booty."

"I know I've made a mess of things but you bringing some random guy to our house is not you Gwen."

"How do you know? It's apparent, I never knew you and maybe you don't know me either. Wait, dang it, I should have brought a girl home to even the playing field. Would that have been better Jacque or is it Jacqueline?"

"Gwen, please don't play with me."

I shrug and he follows me to the bedroom.

"I do know you and this, tonight, isn't the woman I married. This person, the one I see right now, is the old Gwen. She was reckless and dangerous, she'd sleep with any and everybody and she'd bring random men home but not my Gwen. Not the Gwendolyn Page I married."

"NO! You don't get to do that," I tell him beginning to cry. "You don't get to talk me down from the ledge, when you're the reason I'm standing here contemplating jumping. You don't get to comfort me when you're the one who caused my pain. You did this Jacque. YOU!" I begin to hit him. "You broke your promise and I hate you. I HATE YOU!"

"I know," he says grabbing my arms. "I know I did this but I refuse to allow you to go back to that dark place."

"Let me go Jacque," I cry.

"I'm not letting you go. You can hit me, you can scream at me, you can hate me but I'm not about to let you spiral out, not this time."

Jacque

The next morning, I roll over on the couch, in our bedroom, when I hear Gwen beginning to stir. She groans then bolts for the bathroom. When she doesn't come out, I get up to knock on the door but then I hear the shower going. I leave out to get her some orange juice and by the time I get back, she's opening the door.

"Oh my God, you scared me. What are you still doing here?"

"I've been here, since last night. Here," I hand her the juice.

"Jacque, look, I appreciate you being here last night and stopping me from doing something stupid but you can go. I am not in the right headspace to talk to you and I don't have the energy to argue."

The doorbell rings.

"Just get the door and leave me alone." She walks into the closet and I go to see who it is.

"Mark? What are you doing here?" I ask lowering my voice and stepping closer to him.

"You haven't been answering my calls or texts and I was worried. I didn't know if she'd beaten you to death."

"And you thought showing up on my doorstep was the right thing to do?" I ask looking behind me. "You have to go. Now is not a good time."

"What is he doing at my house?"

I close my eyes and cringe.

"He was just leaving," I state.

"No, I wasn't actually," he says pushing pass me. "I came to make sure you hadn't harmed him, you know, with that violent temper you have."

"Why would I need to harm him?"

"Isn't that what you bitter black women do when your man leaves you for someone else? Y'all tear up stuff, bleach clothes, cut tires and stuff. What do you call it Jacque? Ratchet."

"Bitter black women? Ratchet? You're a black woman whisperer now?" Gwen laughs. "Heifer, there is nothing bitter about this black woman but I can get ratchet when the time calls for it. However, allow me to introduce myself. I'm Gwendolyn Page London, a strong black woman who doesn't need to bleach clothes and cut tires. Instead I pay lawyers and cut ties."

"Honey, you might say that but judging by the way you left our offices, I can read between the lines but I'm not going to hold what happened last night against you. We can let bygones be bygones and end on a peaceful not."

Gwen holds up four fingers. "Well, read between these lines and kiss my ass." She laughs, walking over to me like she's about to give me a hug. Instead, she slides her hands into my pajama pants.

"Gwen, what are you doing?" I ask pushing her hands back.

"I'm trying to see if you've had surgery to get a vagina because you don't seem to have a voice when Markesha is around."

"I still have a voice and I am still a man." My voice booms with anger.

"I can't tell since he seems to be speaking for you now. Wait, don't you have a whole wife at home?"

"Don't worry about my household, ma'am. All you need to do is face the fact, Jacque and I will be together, after the dust settles."

"Does it look like I'm kicking up dust by putting up a fight to keep him, little girl? If I'm not mistaken, he was here when I got home last night so maybe you need to tell him, y'all plans to be together. As a matter of fact, I'm glad you're here. Help him get his crap."

"I am not going anywhere Gwen," I snap.

"Mark, you need to leave."

"Yes, you are. You and this little beige heifer need to get out of my house before I call the police."

"I don't have to go anywhere because Jacque belongs to me which means this house belongs to me."

I laugh.

"Mark, please leave and let me handle this. You're making things worse."

"No, she's making everything worse." He says pointing to Gwen. "Why don't you let me have her taken care of? It'll be easy and no one will ever find her body."

I jack him by his collar. "If anything happens to my wife and child, I'll kill you."

"Your what?" Mark questions, pushing me away from him. "She's pregnant? You said you weren't sleeping with her."

"Crazy things happen on vacation, huh?" Gwen says, sitting on the couch.

"You're talking about the vacation that was planned for Jacque and me but I told him to take you instead? That vacation?"

Gwen doesn't say anything.

"Hello! Is that the vacation you're taking about?" Mark laughs.

"In fact it is and I sure do thank you because it was amazing and I'm carrying the proof. Isn't that right Jacque?"

"Mark, it's time for you to go."

Mark laughs. "I'll leave but I will be back for you." He moves to kiss me but I step back.

"Don't come here again," I tell him before shutting the door and turning back to Gwen.

"Not only do you cheat but you're still making me look like a fool. You took me on a vacation you'd planned to take him on. That's why the massages were in the company's name. Wow."

"Gwen, I wasn't thinking. All I was trying to do was save my marriage."

"NO!" She screams. "You were trying to keep up this smokescreen by shutting me up. What happened to you? You told me, last night, my actions weren't the woman you married and neither are yours. You look and speak the same but I don't know who you are."

"I didn't have a choice."

"Jacque, there is always a choice."

"He threatened to fire me."

"And?" She hollers.

"Gwen, you know how long I have worked to get where I am. Everything I've earned, these past three years, is because of the hard work I've put into making it to this level. I am one step away from being a VP and I could not let him come in and snatch it all away."

"And bending him over was more important than your dignity, respect and marriage? Jacque, you're a smart man who can crunch numbers in your sleep. You've made your clients millions of dollars and you thought the only way to handle this was to sleep with your boss? Nah, I'm not buying it. You could have gone to HR and filed a complaint so I know there has to be more. What is it?"

I sigh.

"It's cool, you don't have to be honest with me but you definitely need to be honest with yourself. However, as for this marriage, it's over."

"What about the baby?"

"It's still early enough for an abortion."

Gwen

"Good afternoon, Mrs. London."

"Hey Rachel, it looks like I picked the right day for an appointment."

"Yes, it's been a slow one, for sure, but sign in and I'll get you on back."

I take my seat in the waiting room of Dr. Lea, OBGYN.

"Mrs. London, right this way." Jasmine, her nurse says. "I'm going to get your weight and then you can leave a urine sample."

When I'm done, I am sitting in the room, in a gown freezing.

Knock on the door

"Hey Gwen, how are you today?" Dr. Lea asks.

"I'm good Dr. Lea, how are you?"

"Great, what brings you in today?"

"I took a pregnancy test, it came back positive but I also need to have a full screening for HIV and STDs."

"Okay, I can take care of that for you. When was your last cycle?"

"June, I think."

"Have you been having any cramping, spotting or unusual pains?"

I shake my head, no.

"What about morning sickness?"

"Yes, but it hasn't been bad."

"Okay. Well, lay back and let me examine you."

After an hour, I leave the Dr. Lea's office with a bandaged arm, from them sticking me multiple times for blood and no fix for my broken heart. Getting into the car, I start it and lock the doors while looking at the ultrasound with a March 11, 2019 due date.

I begin to cry.

Jacque and I have never been able to get pregnant. We tried for the first three years of our marriage until I made the decision to stop. It felt like another piece of me was being added to the broken pile, every time the pregnancy test was negative and I couldn't do it anymore. I got on birth control and whenever I ran out, Jacque would use a condom. We'd been careful, up until Hawaii.

I cry harder because I'd gotten comfortable with the possibility of never being a mom. Truth is, when I was younger I decided to never have children because I didn't want him or her to be like me, broken by circumstances you didn't create. My circumstances, growing up without a father because he decided to abandoned us, for another woman. I was thirteen when he broke my heart and it led me to do some disastrous things with my life. It's only because of God's grace that I made it out alive.

Until Jacque.

He changed my thinking because he was excited to be a father and we tried, over and over to get pregnant. When it didn't happen, after year three, I took it as God's sign to move on. I did, well, we did and I was okay with that.

Until now.

I lay my head on the seat, hugging the ultrasound to my chest. The sound of a car horn brings me out of my thoughts. I grab my phone to call Gloria but it rings, instead. Connecting it to the Bluetooth, Gloria's voice booms through the speaker.

"G, what's wrong?" I ask.

"Something happened to mom."

"What do you mean?"

"She wouldn't go into detail but we need to get to her house."

"I'm on the way."

I dry my tears, drop the ultrasound in my purse and hurry to get to my mom's, Georgia's house.

Gloria and I pull up, seconds apart.

"What's going on? Have you talked back to her?" I ask Gloria.

"No, you?"

I shake my head as we walk to the door. Mom opens it.

"Mom, what's wrong?" We both ask.

"Come in."

We walk into the house where she motions for us to follow her into the living room. Turning the corner, Gloria and I stop in our tracks.

"Why is he here?"

"Hey girls," our dad says, standing up with his double-breasted suit and tie freshly starched, looking like the dignified Bishop, he's been playing all these years.

"Mom, what's going on?"

"And is this the emergency you called me about?" Gloria adds.

"Girls, have a seat because your dad needs to talk to you, both, about something."

Reluctant to do so, we both sit.

A few minutes pass in silence.

"I don't know what's going on but I hope the two of you aren't getting back together." I state, meaning every word.

"God no," mom says, "but David has moved back to Memphis."

"Sorry to hear that," I say, "but you could have told us that over the phone."

"There's more," he throws in. "I've been selected as a potential candidate for President of the

National Baptist Convention and part of that will include an intensive investigation into my past."

Gloria and I look at each other.

"Oh," Gloria laughs. "This is about you, like always. What is it David, you don't want people to know the great Bishop David Page abandoned his family for his best friend's wife?"

"It's not like that," he states.

"Yeah, I'm not doing this. I'm out." I tell them.

"Gwendolyn Page, don't you dare!" Mom orders.

"Don't I dare what mother? Walk out on him like he did us? I am not about to sit here and entertain a conversation with this man that has anything to do with helping him. Matter of fact, I don't even understand why you allowed him to come here with this mess."

"He's your father."

"Yea, but only on paper because the man, we knew as our daddy, left us over twenty years ago and never looked back. Not because he was in jail, overseas with the military or strung out on drugs. No, he left us for another woman who happened to be his best friend's wife, who was married to your best friend." I point to mom. "A woman who forbade him from being a father to us while he raised her children and created more.

Now, he has the mitigated gall to show up, out the blue, wanting us to make him look like the Godly man he's lied about all this time. What a joke." I turn to him. "Don't worry daddy, you've never claimed us, we'll return the favor."

"He stands up, with his shoulders back. "Gwen, I know I have no right but—"

"You are correct about that. You have no right but you do have balls. Men! You know what? All y'all make me sick. You think you can just make promises, don't keep them and everything will still be alright.

You vow to love and protect but you don't. You're a bold face liar!" I swipe the tears from my face. "And now, you stand here, with your expensive suit and charming smile and think it's supposed to erase what you've done to us. For years, I allowed what you did to have a hold over me but not anymore. And the way my life is set up, at the moment, all I got is a big screw you!" I grab my purse. "Mom, I love you but don't ever call my number for this man again."

I stomp out the house with Gloria on my heels.

"Sister, wait."

By the time I turn around, my face is covered in tears and I can't speak.

"Gwen, calm down. Breathe."

"I," hard breath, "need," hard breath, "to," hard breath, "go."

"Okay but first calm down." She wraps her arms around me. "Breathe."

When I calm down, Gloria puts me in her car. "We can come back to get your car but for now, you're coming with me."

Thirty minutes later, she and I are walking into her house. She has her arm intertwined with mine and leads me to the den.

"What's going on baby sister because I know it's not about David? You had a full-on panic attack, back there."

"Jacque is having an affair."

"Wait, I don't think I heard you correctly. Say what now?"

She looks at me.

"No G, I don't want pity."

"Girl, this isn't pity. This is pure rage. Let me get some wine because this is some bull!"

Gloria

I walk back into the den with two glasses. "Gwen, how long have you known? I bet he's cheating with some skank at his office too. Who is it? Sasha, his admin? No, it's probably that chick I met at the company picnic. You know the one, with the red lipstick that was all over her teeth. It's her, isn't it?"

"His boss," she corrects me.

"The new boss? Who is she?" I say jumping up to get my laptop. "I'm going to find out who she is and then I'm going to beat her ass and his. What's her name?"

"His name is Mark."

I stop mid step. "I know you lying. Gwendolyn London, I know you are freaking lying."

Tears fall down her face.

"Oh sister," I say, moving close to her. "How did you find out?"

"I showed up at his job to drop off dinner, because he was working late but apparently, his 'working late' was doing his boss. I found them asleep and cuddled in each other's arms."

"Ugh!" I dry heave. "That makes me sick at the stomach."

"The most hurtful part," she says wiping her tears, "I only went to his office to surprise him with news of me being pregnant."

"YOU'RE PREGNANT?"

She shakes her head and I yell so loud, I scare myself and she cries harder.

"That's why you haven't touched your wine. Oh my God."

"After years of trying, we're finally pregnant. I thought it was God's way of giving Jacque and I another chance to start over. I mean, things have been great between us or so I thought." She pauses. "G, I can't believe he did this."

"Girl, forget this! Let's ride because Jacque got you fuc—"

"Yes, he does," she laughs while still crying, cutting me off, "but I'm not ready to do anything yet. For once in my life, I'm going to pray for God's direction before I react."

"Sister, you know I'm all for praying but we can pray after we beat the windows out of his car."

"Slow down," she says pulling me back down on the couch. "G, you know the old me would have already done that, along with slashing tires, bleaching clothes and everything else without caring about going to jail. However, I won't, not this time. I have a business, a brand and a purpose to protect and I refuse to allow Jacque's infidelity to take it away. He took my dignity and a piece of me but I will not allow him to take anything else."

I rub her face.

"You're right Gwen, you have too much to lose. Me, though, I ain't all the way saved and I don't mind going to jail."

"He's not worth it. Anyway, enough about him because I get angry every time I mention his name. Can you believe momma?"

"Girl!! She called me, in a panic, like she'd fallen and couldn't get up. I did ninety miles per hour trying to get to her and she had the nerve to have your daddy sitting there looking pitiful."

"He's your dad too but I get what you're saying."

"We haven't seen or heard from him in over twenty years and he pops up, not asking for forgiveness but expects us to act like he's a doting father, for the sake of his career. Screw him."

"I saw him," Gwen whispers once I'm done with my rant.

"I know, we both did. He was sitting his black tail there, on momma's couch, acting like we saw him yesterday. Girl, forget him and that too little suit. And I'm being nice because I want to use the other f word."

"No, I saw him after he left us."

"When?" I ask her with some confusion.

"When I was eighteen. I went to his house and he slammed the door in my face. He stood there and watched me as I cried on his doorstep, for over thirty minutes but wouldn't let me in. I beat and kicked that door, I screamed his name and still he ignored me. Do you know how small I felt after my own father would do that?"

I lay my head on her shoulder as she cries. We stay that way for a few minutes before I sit up.

"I never told you this but I knew dad was cheating on momma."

"Is that why you hated him?"

"For the most part. I caught him, one day, when I went to his office. He forgot I was coming and I saw them kissing. From that day forward, I couldn't stand him. I went straight home and told momma but she brushed it off."

"Do you think she knew?"

"Yep, she knew but she stayed because her mother stayed with granddaddy. They were passing these generational curses down to us, like candy, because none of them were willing to break it. Momma had two girls and she was willing to put up with David's cheating, for the sake of having a husband. Hell, they are the reason I can't make a relationship work, right now. I sabotage every relationship."

"Hurt them before they hurt you?" Gwen questions and I nod. She continues. "I know all too well. I heard momma tell him, he'd broken my heart before any man could and although I didn't understand it, when I was thirteen, I definitely get it now."

"Gwen, we've got to break this curse. You're pregnant and we cannot continue to let this destroy us. Look at us, we're beautiful and black, educated and enough, financially stable and favored and we got this. Besides, it's almost 2019 and I will not go into the New Year still bound," my voice cracks. "I'm tired of being alone. I want a warm body lying next to me at night and someone to wake up too, in the morning. I want my own relationship."

This time she hugs me.

"I agree and that's exactly what I'm going to do. I love Jacque but he isn't mine to keep and before I go through years of misery, I'll rather spend every minute alone."

"Amen to that."

"I have an idea. Let's go out of town for New Years," Gwen suggests. "Jacque and I had plans to go to Gatlinburg but I can change it. And seeing, we're our own boss, we can stay as long as we want."

"I am down for that but promise me something."

"What?"

"You will give yourself time to heal instead of going back to the dark place that almost killed you before. Promise me, you'll talk to someone, if you feel yourself spiraling. You have a baby to think about, this time."

"I promise but I don't know if I'm keeping this baby."

Jacque

Knock on the door

"What can I do for you, Mark?"

"You can start by thanking me," he says closing the door.

"For what?"

"For covering your ass."

"What are you talking about?"

"All the damage your wife did to our offices. I had to pay, Jules, the head of maintenance and Mario, in IT a total of five thousand dollars to work over the weekend to clean up the mess she caused." He says looking around. "It was worth it because you can't even tell anything was wrong."

"I didn't ask you to do that because I was ready to tell Mr. Graft the truth but you said, you'd handle it."

"I did because I knew paying him was better than losing our jobs. Besides, we both know money has the power to do anything. Well, that and good sex," he laughs. "Now, say thank you Mark or you can just give me a kiss—with tongue."

"Mark, I am not in the mood for your dramatics and I will not be kissing you today or ever."

"My, aren't we testy this afternoon. You know I can help you with that." He says getting ready to walk around my desk.

"No! I have work to do."

He slams my laptop closed almost catching my hands. "I know exactly what work you have but you owe me. Do you know what I could have done with five thousand dollars?"

"That's not my problem. We would have never been in this predicament had it not been for you."

He laughs. "Are you seriously blaming me? Dude, give me a break. You could have ignored my advances but instead you chose to bend me over my desk. If anybody is to blame, it's you. My wife didn't catch us, remember."

"Your wife doesn't care and my wife wouldn't have caught us either, if I would have left on time."

"Oh, did I tell you to fall asleep? It looks to me, you wanted her to find out."

"Not like this."

"I'm sorry your little wife found out, the way she did, but now that she knows, great. You can get an apartment; we can stop sneaking into hotels and move on with our lives."

"Move on with our lives, are you serious? Dude, you're still going home to your wife."

"That's only until I can get her to agree to the divorce and you know this."

"NO!" I say standing up. "What I know is, my life is a mess right now and I can't do this anymore. We're done Mark."

"Stop being silly. You're just emotional but it'll all blow over in a few weeks. Give what's her name time and she'll forgive you. They always do," he smiles.

"I don't have time to see if this blows over. My wife is pregnant and I'm going to do everything I can to get her to forgive me, now, so that she can have a great pregnancy."

He rolls his eyes. "Why?

"What do you mean?"

"Look Jacque, you know I don't want any children and I'm not about to play gay stepdad with yours. I don't care how sexy you look naked. Besides, we both know you're not father material so cut your losses now before you get attached."

"I wasn't giving you a choice. This is my life and whatever I decide to do, with my child, will be my choice and not yours." I walk towards the door. "It's time for you to get your ass out of my office."

"Jacque, baby calm down. I was just kidding. We can figure this out."

"No, there is no longer a 'we' when it comes to you and me. We're done."

"Jacque, you can't be serious."

"Get out Mark and from now on, if it doesn't pertain to work, don't bother coming in here."

"I'm going to leave, only because you're in your feelings," he says, "but I'll be by the hotel tonight to help you relax."

Before I can respond, there is a knock on the door.

"Mr. London, I am sorry to bother you but you may want to look at this email."

"Can it wait, Sasha?" Mark demands.

"Mr. London," she says passing me her iPad and rolling her eyes at Mark. "You need to see this."

Subject: After Hours

Dear Board of Directors, CEO, COO and everybody else;

I thought you'd like to know what is happening, in that big beautiful building, you pay for ... AFTER HOURS. I should warn you though, this video is graphic. Enjoy!

Signed,

A Whistle Blower.

I click on the attachment and my mouth drops.

"What is it?" Mark asks but I am too stunned to answer. "Jacque, what is it."

When the video begins to play, it's of me and Mark, in his office. His face is blurred out but mine is seen clearly. The sound is turned up on the iPad so you can hear us kissing, breathing hard and Mark's disguised voice, screaming for me to—

"AH!" I yell, throwing the iPad into the wall.

Sasha and Mark, both jump.

"Good, you're both here." I look up to see the owner of the company, John Graft, standing there. "Sasha, can you excuse us?"

"Yes sir." She closes the door behind her.

"I'm guessing by that shattered iPad you've seen the video?"

"John, I can explain," Mark stutters.

"You can explain why a video of your direct report, with his ass out while bending another man over a desk, in my corporate headquarters, is playing all over the internet? Go ahead because I'd love to hear it."

"I-uh, I wasn't aware there was a video sir."

"No, I guess you weren't but let me cut to the chase. While I am all for people being themselves and loving who they want to love, I'll be damned, if I allow it to ruin the reputation of the company my father built."

"John, I am so sorry," I tell him.

"Who was the other person?" He questions. "Is he an employee too?"

I look back at Mark whose face is turning beet red.

"No sir," I say. "But I am very sorry this happened and I can promise, it will never happen again."

"I believe you and normally that would be enough for me to only suspend you but giving the magnitude of this, you're fired and have one hour to get off the property. Mark, I need to see you, now!"

He leaves and Mark starts to say something.

"Get out!" I seethe before walking in circles. "Damn it!"

I rush to my desk to call Gwen before she sees the video. When she doesn't answer, I send a text.

ME: Gwen, please call me. It's important.

Gwen

Still at Gloria's, we're in the middle of cooking when my phone vibrates with a call from Jacque. Ignore.

He sends a text.

> JACQUE: Gwen, please call me. It's important.

"Jacque?" Gloria questions.

"Yes, talking about call him, it's important."

"Go ahead and I can watch the sauce."

"Girl, forget Jacque. I am not in the mood for whatever it is, he deems important."

She shrugs and I put my phone on do not disturb. We finish cooking then we go back into the living room to watch an episode of New Amsterdam.

24 years ago

"Girls, your mom and I want to talk to you." Dad said looking from me to Gloria. "I don't know another way to say this but," he pauses, "your mom and I are getting a divorce."

"What?" I yell, jumping up from the chair. "NO! You promised you wouldn't leave us."

"Gwen, baby calm down," mom says grabbing my hand. "We tried to make it work but we can't."

"Gwen, listen to me. I am still your dad and you'll always be my girl," he says wiping my tears, "and just because I won't be living here, it doesn't mean our relationship will change."

"You promise?"

"He's lying!" Gloria screams. "Tell the truth daddy. You have a whole other family and as soon as you walk out that door, you'll never be back."

"Stop lying!" I yell at her. "Daddy, tell her."

"Gloria, you're out of line," mom scolds.

"No, you're out of line for allowing him to lie to us. Momma, you know he's lying and he's going to break Gwen's heart, leaving us to pick up the pieces. He's already got us looking like fools at church because everybody knows he's sleeping with Marjorie."

"Gloria, I know you're upset but you need to stay in a child's place." Daddy states.

"I'm sixteen years old," she says stepping to him, "and I'm more of an adult than you'll ever be. No adult would have an affair with his wife's best friend while proclaiming to be a man of God. I'm going to Jennifer's house."

She stomps out and I turn back to my parents.

"Daddy," I cry.

"Baby girl, I promise to be here for you. For birthdays, graduations, marriages and the birth of my *grandchildren. I'm not leaving you and you can come visit me whenever you want."*

"You promise?"

"I promise," he says holding out his pinky finger.

A YEAR LATER

I'd been up, for hours, because it's my thirteenth birthday and daddy is coming to pick me up. My bag is packed and my stomach is full of butterflies. It's been six months since I've seen him because momma stopped going to the church when they announced their divorce.

"Gwen, your dad is here," mom yells.

"Coming."

I grab my bag and bounce down the hall.

"Daddy," I squeal.

"Happy Birthday baby girl."

He tries to sound happy but his face is saying something else.

"Daddy, what's wrong?"

He takes my hand and we go over to the couch.

"I know I promised you could come home with me, this weekend, but Marjorie is sick and not up for company."

"But I'm not company, daddy, I'm your daughter." I say releasing his hand.

"I know but I don't want you getting sick, too."

"How can she catch morning sickness?" Gloria says from behind me. "Isn't that what she's sick with daddy?"

"She's pregnant?" I ask him, tears springing from my eyes.

He doesn't answer.

"You're a liar!" I scream to daddy. "You said our relationship wouldn't change and it has. I don't talk to you anymore and I haven't seen you in six months." My voice trails off. "It's my birthday and you promised," I cry.

"David, it's time for you to go," mom tells him, placing her hands on my shoulders. I turn into her and cry while she pats my back. "Stay here and let me talk to your father."

He tries to touch me but I move away and when they walk out, I go over to the door.

"You are one sorry bastard. It's one thing to cheat on me with your best friend's wife but it's an entirely different thing to break your daughter's heart. That girl loves you and never finds fault, in YOU and this is how you do her."

"Georgia, I'm sorry but I have to do what's best for my wife and right now, she needs calm and rest."

"Calm and rest?" She laughs. "I didn't say anything when you decided we could no longer be a part of the church, I helped you established. I didn't say one word, when you disrespected me, in public. I never opened my mouth when you walked out on us but I'll be damned if I allow you to hurt my children. We didn't ask for this. You are the one who couldn't keep his penis to himself."

"I know, got-damn-it, I know and I'm sorry."

"Yea but not sorry enough to stop breaking your daughters' heart. You do know you're setting them up for a lifetime of heartache, right?"

"Georgia, I'll make it up to them."

"No, you won't because the only thing you've made them is broken. Get off my property and if you can't do right by your flesh and blood, don't bring your sorry, black ass back here."

After that day, the only time I saw my dad was when he was on TV. He moved to Oklahoma, a few years afterwards and never looked back. Those graduations, birthdays and marriages, he promised to be there for ... he never did.

My mom was right though. He'd left me broken.

I open my eyes, not remembering where I am until I see Gloria asleep on the other couch. I look at my watch and see it's almost midnight. I wipe the tears, I hadn't realized were falling, from my face before I wake Gloria. It's hard because she drank an entire bottle of wine and she sleeps heavy.

I never realized, until now, how much she was affected by the absence of our father because I was too consumed with hating him. After that last visit to his house, I was hell bent on wiping him from my memories and I never stopped to ask how she was dealing with everything. I assumed, she was strong enough to get through it, without me because she acted as if it hadn't hurt her like it did me but now, I know, she's broken too.

"Come on sister, let's get you to bed."

When she's finally in bed, I shower and put on some pajamas I got from her room. Getting my phone, I plug it into the charger and climb into the guest bed.

Once it powers on, I see more text messages from Jacque. I delete the entire thread without reading them.

Opening Pandora, I press play on the Gospel Channel and a song, I'd never heard, begins to play. I lay the phone on the nightstand and press my back into the headboard.

"In the book of Matthew, fourth chapter around the third verse, Jesus was tempted by Satan while He was at His weakest time. Every time Satan came with his confusion and temptations, Jesus would respond only in scripture. He did this to show us that we, too, can respond in scripture. There is power in His word and power in His name." *The man says before the song plays.* *"The doctor may have given you a bad report but Isaiah 41:10 says, do not fear because I am with you and do not be dismayed because I will strengthen you. He gave us power, healing power, living power and power to save."*

"I've got power, over the enemy. Speak it and things start to change," *the lady sings.* *"Dominion, authority; whatever you need, there's power in Jesus name."*

While the song plays, I allow the tears to fall and I pray.

"God, I need you and you have permission to have your way in my life. Whatever your will is, I surrender because I need your power to heal and be restored. I'm tired of carrying this anger, I'm tired of being broken and I'm tired of trying to fill a void that only you can fill. Help me God. Cut away anything that is not for my good and destroy whatever I am not strong enough to walk away from. God, I surrender. Amen."

Gloria

I roll over and the light from outside causes me to cuss under my breath. "I really need to get some darker curtains," I mumble while squeezing my eyes shut. The pain is reminding me why I must stop drinking.

I reach over into the nightstand to get two Advil and the bottle of water I had sitting there. Taking the pills, I grab my phone and open Facebook.

"Dang," I say when I see all the notifications and inbox messages. I click on the first one, from a girl I went to college with. I press play and sit straight up in the bed.

"Oh my, oh my God!"

I get up and my foot gets caught in the comforter. I'm dancing around trying to get loose before running out of my bedroom and into the kitchen.

"Dang-it," Gwen says spilling her coffee and pulling the headphones from her ear. "You almost gave me a heart attack. What's wrong with you?"

"I almost fell when my foot got caught in my comforter," I tell her trying to catch my breath. "Forget that. Have you been on social media?"

"No, I've been checking emails because I'm so behind at the office. I had to send some additional information to Jocelyn pertaining to the pending contracts for the Ross and Livingston clients. Then I had to schedule an appointment to walk through the house over on Spartan St. and another for an inspection that's overdue on Delaware."

I'm standing there, waving my hand for her to hurry up and finish.

"Are you done?"

"Yes, Ms. Rude. What were you trying to say?"

"I wasn't trying to say anything. Here," I hand her my phone. "You have to see this for yourself."

She puts the coffee cup down, on the kitchen's island, and takes the phone.

"Click on the video."

"Okay, calm down."

"Child, you will not believe the news we got yesterday. An employee of Graft Enterprises was caught with his pants down, literally. This morning, here at Speak Up Woman, we received a video of two men going at it, at their job. Baby, you'd thought they were filming for a porn site. Our source identified the man as Managing Director, Jacque London. Now, we don't have the name of the other male but we, at Speak Up Woman, will not stop until we get it. I guess working late has taken on a whole new meaning." She and the other host laughs. "Anyway, see for yourself but I have to warn you, the video is pretty graphic so if you're in a communal space, you may want to turn your volume down."

The video switches and Gwen's hand flies to her mouth as the air fills with the sound of Jacque and who I know to be Mark having sex.

"Where did you get this?" She asks as the tears begin to fill her eyes. "Facebook? Is it all over the internet for everybody to see?"

I shake my head, yes.

"Oh my God! Please turn it off," she yells, pushing the phone towards me.

I'm fumbling with it and their moans are getting louder and more vocal, while she's screaming, turn it off.

"I'm trying."

"AHHH! Why would he do this to me?" She screams, picking up the coffee cup and slamming it against the counter.

I grab her arm but she snatches it away.

"Gwen, stop! Baby stop, because you're bleeding."

She slides down to the floor.

I turn her arm over and see a deep gash at the base of her hand, near her wrist. It still has a chunk of the cup lodged in it.

"Hold still. Gwen, listen to me and hold your hand right here while I get a towel."

I rush to the bathroom and snatch a towel. When I turn the corner, Gwen is just staring ahead, holding the piece of cup.

"Oh my God! Girl, I told you to sit still, not to pull the freaking glass out."

"G, why would he do this?" She cries.

"I don't know sister."

"Everybody will see it and know my husband is gay. Oh my God."

"Gwen, please be still. I need to stop the bleeding."

She pushes me away. "Just let me die because it has to be better than this."

"The devil is a lie! You are not going to die, not today and not on my watch."

"I can't keep going through this," she cries, "it hurts too much. He promised not to hurt me G."

"I know baby but right now, you're losing too much blood. I need to get you to the hospital."

"He promised," her words beginning to slur.

***

"Hey, how are you feeling?" I ask Gwen when I see her eyes open.

"Where am I?"

"The hospital."

She looks confused.

"You cut your arm with that coffee cup. You lost a lot of blood and the doctors had to perform surgery to repair the tendon in your wrist."

She raises her arm and cries. I pull the chair next to her bed and grab her hand.

"It hurts." I cry.

"I can ask the nurse to give you something."

"I meant my heart."

"Just tell me what you need to get through this," I say squeezing her hand. "Just tell me sister."

"I gave this man twelve years of my life and all I ever required of him was honesty. He knows my past. He knows how broken I was and he promised to never make me feel like that and he did. He broke me all over again."

Her cry turns into sobs. "How could he? He was sleeping with me and that man. He said he loved me and would never hurt me like this. He broke—"

She begins to gasp.

"Breathe Gwendolyn. Breathe."

"I can't—I can't."

"Help," I holler grabbing her face.

The nurses and a doctor come running in.

"She can't breathe."

"Mrs. London, you're having a panic attack. Breathe." The nurse coaches. "Good, now in and out. Come on, you can do it."

I hear them talking but then my eyes get heavy.

Gwen

A few days later, I'm at home on the couch, trying to do the hand exercises I was taught before I left the hospital. I have a splint on my arm that I have to wear for up to six weeks. The pain, is bad at times and being pregnant, I can't anything stronger than Tylenol. Nonetheless, I'm surviving.

The doorbell rings.

"I got it." Gloria calls out from the kitchen.

I hear her talking but can't make out who she's talking too.

"Sister, look whose here."

I look up to see our Pastor, Magnolia Reeves from High Point. "Pastor Magnolia, what are you doing here?"

"Can't a pastor come and check on two of her favorite members?"

I stand up and give her a hug.

"Of course, you're always welcome here."

"Glad to hear it because when one of us is hurt, we all hurt." She states, taking a seat next to me.

"I hope I'm not catching you all at a bad time but I wanted to stop and see how you were doing after Gloria told me about the accident. How are you feeling?"

"I'm good," I lie.

"You don't have to pretend with me Gwen. I've been in a dark place before and the only way I escaped, I had to face what I was running from. You all know some of the things I faced last year. I wouldn't have made it without recognizing and coming to terms with what was chasing me."

"How did you do it?" I inquire.

"Therapy," she smiles. "I'm not ashamed to say that my issues superseded what I could do on my own. Don't misunderstand, I am an advocate for prayer and fasting but sometimes your flesh needs help too. My therapist was great and she opened my eyes to see that all I needed to do, to stop being chased, was to stop running. That's why I brought you something."

She hands me a book. "This is a journal, called Be a Fighter. When I was going through my storm, my therapist gave me a journal titled HERoine Addict and I didn't realize how therapeutic writing was until I began doing it. Anyway, it helped me, a lot and the same author created this one too."

"You're an addict?" Gloria blurts.

Pastor Magnolia laughs. "I used to be but not to pills and alcohol. I was addicted to fear."

"I don't understand. Why would your therapist give you a journal about heroin?"

"No, it's not the drug heroin. It's H-E-R-O-I-N-E," she spells out, "a female hero or a woman who is admired. The author took the letters of heroine and broke them down into the words; habitable, embody, refine, outward, inward, notwithstanding and effectual in a way to help the reader begin their journey to destiny."

"Oh," Gloria and I say together.

"It's great and in Be a Fighter, she simply encourages you to fight and that's all I want you to do. Gwen, I don't know all that you're battling with, inwardly but will you be a fighter?"

"I don't know how," I tell her as the tears begin.

"The first step is calling out what you've been trying to fight on your own because knowing what it is, gives you the power to destroy it. Gwen, you're stronger than you give yourself credit for and you can overcome this but you can't give up. No matter how hard it is, you've got to fight."

"Thank you, Pastor."

"I left the name and number of my therapist, in the back of the journal. Start there, without the shame and after you start the fight, I'll bring you a copy of HERoine Addict."

"Thank you."

"No thanks needed but can we pray?"

I sit while they both touch me.

"Dear God, thank you for your protection over our sister and thank you for being so generous with your grace and mercy. Now God, I ask for your ear because Gwen needs you. She's hurt, broken, confused and in a dark place but I know you to be better than any power company when it comes to restoring power. So, God I ask for you to touch, right now. God, I need you to do like you did Jeremiah at the potter's house and restore the clay.

She's been tarnished by the world but you can transform. Forgive her transgressions, forgive her for thinking her pain was bigger than your purpose and forgive her for thinking she's broken beyond repair. God, we stand in the gap, for her, refusing to let her die in the pit. All we need is strength to pull her out because we're willing.

God, she may have hit some bumps but she can bounce back. She may have some stitches but she can still speak. She may have been left broken but you God, you can work miracles with broken pieces and we say, have your way. Reshape the clay God that you have in your hands, making her into the masterpiece we know her to be. And God, we may never be able to thank you enough but let our faithfulness and gratefulness be acceptable unto you. God, we close this prayer, saying much obliged. Amen."

"Amen."

"Thank you for coming Pastor."

"It was my pleasure. Please call me, if there is anything I can do. God bless you both."

She hugs the both of us before Gloria walks her out.

"Sister, thank you for calling pastor."

"You never have to thank me but let's heal together, okay?"

Jacque

I pull up at home, nervous about going in. It's been a few days since I've talked to Gwen and I'm sure she knows about the video because it's all over the internet. What scares me is, she hasn't called or answered any of my texts.

I press the garage door opener and it surprises me that it still works. I turn off the car and walk inside, to see Gwen and Gloria standing in the kitchen.

"You got some nerve," Gloria barks at me. "How dare you show up here after everything you've done? You nasty, no good, useless mother—"

Gwen touches her on the arm. "G, I got this."

"No sister, let me beat his ass, bust the windows out his truck or something."

"Slow down Jasmine Sullivan, because we are not about to bust no windows or beat anybody's ass. Not yet anyway," I reply looking at Jacque.

"He owes us an explanation Gwen. We let this," she says with her mouth scrunched and looking him up and down, "whatever he is, into our lives."

"Gloria, I'm sorry but this is between me and my wife. She is the only one I married and owe an explanation too." I tell her.

"You sure because that video, circulating all over the internet, clearly shows you in a tri-relationship with my sister and your boss? At least he had the decency to cover his face. So, tell me, buddy-in-law, did you explain anything to him while you were making gay porn videos?"

"Gay porn videos?" He repeats. "I haven't made any videos. I didn't even know that one was out there."

"Well it is and the whole freaking world has seen it."

Gwen looks at her. "G, can you give us a few minutes?"

When she walks away from Gwen, I notice the wrap on her arm causing me, out of instinct, to go to her.

"Babe, what happened to your arm?"

She pulls away. "Please don't call me that."

"Can I, at least, ask if you're okay?"

"Oh yes Jacque, I'm great. I'm pregnant by a gay man who has a video that's viral on the internet. I guess, I should be grateful the only thing you did give me was a baby and not HIV or a STD. Do you know how embarrassing it is to have to ask your doctor to test you, for everything, because your husband can't be faithful?"

"I've apologized Gwen. What more do you want?"

"I can think of a few things but you may not like them."

"Look, I didn't come to argue with you but we need to talk. You don't have to be so cold."

"I don't have to be so cold? Says the man who has a video all over the freaking internet. Do you know how many of my customers have called me about this? Do you know how embarrassing it is?"

"Yes, you've said that over and over but it's also embarrassing for me too."

"Yea, well, screw you because I didn't do it to you. Jacque, you really hurt me but more than anything, you broke me."

"Stop being so dramatic," I snap. "I am not the one who broke you. You had daddy issues long before I came along. If anything, I helped you."

"Wow," she laughs. "Are you really going to stand here and blame my daddy issues for you being gay? I didn't make you cheat sweetie; your desires did."

"I'm sorry. I shouldn't have said that because you are not to blame. It's been a long few days."

"That you're right about, dear husband. Yes, I have daddy issues but I was honest with you about them and never took them out on you. I begged you to walk away from me, twelve years ago but you stayed, promising to be here. You confessed your love and took vows before God to cherish and honor me. You said you'd forsake all others and that death would be the only thing to part us. YOU PROMISED THAT! Not my got-damn daddy!"

"Gwen, I made a mistake and I'm trying to fix it."

"A mistake?" She repeats. "No Jacque. A mistake is getting the wrong brand of bread, putting salt in your coffee instead of sugar or wearing a black and blue sock. Those are mistakes that can be easily fixed but what you did, that was a choice. A choice you made every time you had sex with that man then came home to me. When you laid, cuddled in bed with me, after being with that man, it was a choice. When you looked me in my face and lied, it was a choice. A choice YOU made so please don't play me Jacque because I'm not that naïve twenty-eight-year-old, you met twelve years ago. Baby, I'm full grown and capable of telling the difference between chocolate and bull and this my dear is not chocolate."

"I'm not playing you Gwen and you're right, it was a choice. One that I deeply regret but you must know, it was never my intent to hurt you. Yes, I should have been honest with you but I didn't know how."

"By opening your mouth and admitting your flaws. Jacque, none of us are perfect but had somebody come to me, saying my husband was gay; I would have gone to my grave calling them a liar. But I guess, the jokes on me, huh? Man, I was a fool."

"Baby, this isn't on you."

"No, your cheating isn't but being hurt is because I allowed you into a space I had closed off. I allowed you to penetrate parts of me I knew could be easily broken. I gave you me, Jacque, the real me because you said you could handle it." She pauses as tears spill from her eyes. "You told me I could trust you and I did. I trusted you with the ugliness of my past and even with secrets I haven't had the courage to tell my sister. And you were lying this entire time. But I must give it to you, if I could clap I would because you were great at pretending."

"Gwen, I wasn't pretending. The man you married, that's who I am. I love you and I never intended to hurt you."

"And you didn't have too, had you been honest. How long have you known you were gay?"

I sigh before sitting at the kitchen's island.

"Since I was eight."

"Wow."

"I never acted on them though. Not until Jimmy."

"Who is Jimmy?"

"My mother's husband. When they first got married, he acted like he cared for me but then he noticed I was different. I didn't want to play sports, like my older brother and he said I carried myself in a feminine way. In public, he despised me but in private, he desired me.

He never acted on them but he would touch me and watch me, when he thought I was asleep. When I turned eleven, he started making me go on his fishing and camping trips with his boys. He said it would make me a man. I didn't think anything of it because some of his friends had boys too, the same age. What I didn't know was, they also shared the same fetish for little boys."

I stop to control my emotions.

"The first two years, the trip was good. For my thirteenth birthday, we packed the car with our camping and fishing gear, as usual. We all met, at the camp site and things were like they always were until we got ready to put up our tents. Usually, me and the two other boys, would be in one big tent but this time; it was different. Jimmy called us around the fire and told us we'd be playing a game. He put a bowl in front of us that had different color poker chips and we each had to take one. I pulled the red one.

The color chip determined what tent we had to go into. It still never clicked what was happening until I was inside the red tent, getting my sleeping bag out. Jimmy's friend, Wayne, came in and when he zipped up the tent, I asked what he was doing and he said, explaining the rules of the game. The rules; don't fight, don't scream, don't tell and take one for the team."

"Oh my God."

I shake my head to clear the memories.

"Did you ever tell?" She asks.

"Once but my mom told me to keep my mouth closed because it meant she'd have to give up all he did for us. She knew but kept sending me with Jimmy and the first trip, after I told, he beat me so bad that I was in the hospital for seven days. He told the police, I'd fallen off a small cliff while playing."

"What happened to the other boys?"

"One of them committed suicide, a few years ago."

"And the other one?"

I don't say anything.

"Jacque, what happened to the other boy?"

"He grew up to become my boss. The third boy is Mark."

Gwen

"Damn!" Gloria says causing me and Jacque to jump. "I'm sorry, I didn't mean to interrupt but Gwen, we're going to be late if we don't leave in twenty minutes. Y'all can finish your conversation and I'll go back to listening from the door."

I look at her and she shrugs before walking out.

"Why didn't you ever tell me this?"

"Then I would have to admit that I'm broken too. Would you have married me had you known?"

"I don't know but it should have been my choice Jacque. Have you been with other men, since we've been married?"

"No! I promise."

"Then why now?"

"I hadn't seen Mark in years until he showed up at my job, as my new VP. He was married so I thought he'd dealt with the demons of the past but the more time we spent together, the closer we got. He would flirt and I'd resist but one night, while working late, we slept together."

"The moment you started sleeping with him, you should have been honest with me."

"I didn't know how. You were so damaged, from your past and I knew the moment I told you, you'd spiral and I didn't want to be the reason."

"What makes you think I would have? Sure, I would have been heartbroken but I could have handled it better than finding out like this. Look at me Jacque," I say holding up my arm. "This last week has been pure hell."

"Do you think my week has been a bed of roses? My face is the one that has gone viral and I'm the one who lost my job."

"Well, actions do have consequences," I shrug. "Jacque, I get that we've both had our share of problems and I am sorry for all you went through, as a child, but it doesn't excuse what you've done. Maybe, we both tried to be for each other what we couldn't be for ourselves and somewhere along the way, we got good at pretending. Whatever the case, I think we could both benefit from going to counseling, separately."

I walk over to the journal from Pastor Reeves. I take a piece of paper and write down the therapist's name. "Here, this is a number for a therapist."

"Thanks, and Gwen, I never intended for any of this to happen."

"No one ever does."

"Will it be okay if I get some clothes?"

"Yeah, just be gone by the time I get home."

I call for Gloria because I knew she was standing around the corner.

"Gwen, thank you for not judging me." I tell her.

"Who am I to judge when I have skeletons in my closet too? Besides, I don't have a heaven or hell to send you so it's not for me to judge." I grab my purse.

"Wait, may I ask about the baby? Is it mine?"

I open my mouth but no words come out.

"Hold up, little Richard," Gloria says coming around the corner. "So, because you stick your little nasty penis in other people, you assume my sister cheats?"

"No, that's not what I meant. Gwen, I'm only asking because we both know you couldn't get pregnant in the first three years of our marriage and now you are. Added with the fact, you were just with some man, whose name you didn't know, the other night."

"Wow. After having a half-way decent conversation, you ruin it with stupidity. For the record, jackass, I have never broken our vows. The other night, was a lapse in judgment, after catching you asleep in another man's arm but you know I didn't sleep with him. And if I had, he still wouldn't be the daddy."

"I'm sorry but I needed to be sure."

"And I need you to be sure you're not here when I get back."

Gloria mumbles something under her breath and I'm sure she's calling him all kinds of names.

"The nerve of him to think I was cheating," I rant slamming Gloria's car door.

Gloria pulls out the driveway and continues to drive until I stop talking.

"Um sister, you care to tell me about this man you had in your house?"

I look at her.

"I was stupid and had a lapse in logical thinking because I was angry at Jacque but I didn't sleep with him."

"You brought him back to your house though."

"I said I wasn't thinking G!" I yell. "Yes, it was careless and I could have done something I would have regretted but I didn't."

"I'm sorry," she says touching my hand. "Calm down."

"I just don't know what to do."

"We're going to go to church, get delivered and then make an appointment with the therapist Pastor Magnolia recommended."

Women's Conference

Walking into High Point, it's already crowded.

"Come on," Gloria says. "Demetria is holding our seats up front."

We walk down the aisle to the pew behind Pastor Reeves and the ministerial staff. She looks back and smiles. The praise team is up singing and before I can get to my seat, the tears have already started.

"You know my name. You know my name. You know my name, hmm. You know my name and oh how you comfort me. And oh, how you counsel me. It still amazes me that I am your friend. So now, I pour out my heart to you, yea, here in your presence I am made new. So now, I pour out my heart to you. I give you my heart, Lord, here in your presence I am made new."

I stand and raise my hands.

"No fire can burn me, no battle can turn me, no mountain can stop me cause you hold my hand. I'm walking in your victory cause your power is within me. No giant can defeat me cause you hold my hand."

By the time the song is over, I am a mess. Gloria hands me some tissue as I take my seat.

"Hello ladies!" Pastor Magnolia says to the packed sanctuary. "I hope you came tonight with worship and deliverance in mind."

"Oh yes!" Voices reply.

"I know this is the first time we've had this type of conference, here at High Point, but God placed it on my heart last year and I had to be obedient. I realized, through all my struggles that disobedience was killing my purpose and for me to be what you all needed, I had to survive me. Therefore, I named this conference, surviving me."

"Amen," the congregation says.

"Surviving me, may be a strange name, for a conference, but sometimes the thing that is killing us, isn't sickness or disease but it's us. As women, we take on and endure so much. We deal with daddy issues, un-forgiveness, heartbreak, brokenness, low self-esteem and unworthiness; all while being a sister, friend, wife, mother and sometimes pastor. But tonight, I declare no more. Tonight, women of God, we are coming out and it starts by Surviving Me. Somebody say, surviving me."

"Surviving me," the crowd shouts.

"Yesssss God," Someone yells.

"Bible shares in Colossians two, verses thirteen through fifteen, *'you were dead because of your sins and because your sinful nature was not yet cut away. Then God made you alive with Christ, for he forgave all our sins. He canceled the record of the charges against us and took it away by nailing it to the cross. In this way, he disarmed the spiritual rulers and authorities. He shamed them publicly by his victory over them on the cross.'* Tonight, tell yourself, I will survive me."

"I will survive me," we all say.

"Hallelujah!"

"Praise you God!"

The praise team takes the stage again. After two songs, a welcome, fellowship period and offering; tonight's speaker was introduced.

Her name is Prophetess Geneses Warren, someone I'd hear of but never had the privilege to hear, in person.

Thirty minutes in and she is slaying the crowd, casting out demons, speaking in tongue and prophesying. I am standing in awe of this bold woman of God as she walks the crowd. Watching her with tears streaming down my face, she stops in front of me.

"Woman of God, tonight, you're going to leave here whole. The daddy issues, will be no more because we're taking your power back. Is this your sister?"

I nod.

"You're going to be free too. See, you're used to being rejected but the only way you can be delivered from the spirit of rejection, you must first admit that you're rejected. I don't care who's trying to defame your character, who's gossiping about you or what has happened recently; it's all because of the manifestations of rejection. I need both of you to hear me.

Rejection is a dangerous spirit and it will cause you to do harm to you and anybody you seek to love. No more. You are more than what rejection says. You are worthy of being loved and you are worthy of being made whole but you've first got to admit it. Are you ready?"

"Yes," I cry. "I'm tired."

She places the microphone to my mouth.

"Declare from your mouth."

"I'm rejected."

She places the microphone to Gloria's mouth.

"I'm rejected," she repeats.

"Not anymore. Tonight, by the confessions of your own mouths, your ransom has been paid and you can come out. Tonight, sisters, God has given me permission to change your name from rejected to redeemed. You are free to go for I am saying to you what God said to Joshua. Today, I have rolled away the shame of your slavery. You are free. Can I get some women, who have been where they are but survived, to surround them?"

When Gloria and I are in the center of the many women, she begins to pray.

"God, as we stand on the altar tonight, we thank you. We thank you for giving us the wisdom to call on you in our time of need and we thank you for being a prayer away. God, thank you for giving us access to your never yielding power. Now God, as we stand under an open heaven, we ask you to have your way in this house.

God, I'm calling on you tonight for the broken women on this altar and those in the pews, who need your touch. Father, they can't leave here the same, not on our watch and if I must pray until midnight, I'll do it. I'm standing here, now, decreeing they shall be free.

No God, they must be freed for they've been in hell too long. They've overstayed their welcome, in darkness and I need you to turn on the light. They've been in the pit, too long, and I need for you to drop a rope to pull them up. God, put your word on their tongue so every time they speak, mountains move.

Put power in their feet so every place they step, they leave your anointing. God, they are your children and tonight they shall be restored and redeemed. By your power Lord, by your might and by your word; we ask. Amen."

Gwen

Gloria and I get in the car, after the service, fasten our seatbelts and sit there.

"Wow," she says. "I've never experienced worship like this. I mean, Pastor Magnolia is great but this, this was mind blowing."

"Me either and I get what you're saying. The entire service was amazing but sister, it made me realize something."

"What's that?" She asks, starting the car and pulling off.

"I've been down too long and I'm tired. I know I've said this before but I want better and the only way I get better, I must do something different than what I've been doing. I'm no longer accepting what can satisfy my now because I'm making a conscious decision to protect me and my sanity."

"You go girl!"

"I want it for you too," I tell her. "Do you remember what you told me? We're beautiful and smart but we've allowed brokenness to stand in our way. It's time to survive ourselves and to make sure I don't back out, I'm going to call the therapist on tomorrow."

She doesn't reply and I don't push but when we pull up to my house, she puts the car in park and I realize she's crying.

"G? What's wrong?"

"I'm gay."

"You're—wow. I, um—how, I know how but when? Why didn't you tell me? Dang G, I thought we didn't have secrets."

"I fully came to terms with it, a few months ago so I haven't been keeping it from you long. I was just finding my own footing and after tonight, I realized that I, too, am tired. I'm gay."

"Good for you," I tell her grabbing the door handle.

"Speaking of secrets, I heard what you said to Jacque. What haven't you told me?"

I sigh. "There's a lot I need to tell you but not tonight. I'll talk to you on tomorrow."

"You're not mad at me, are you?"

I have one leg out the car but I turn back to her. "No G, I'm not mad. Am I disappointed that you didn't share this with me, yes but not mad? You have a right to live your life by whatever tempo you set and if that means, you loving women, so be it. You're my big sister and I love you, for you."

"Thank you and I love you too."

"Text me when you make it home."

I press the code into the security box and open the garage. I stop when I see Jacque's truck parked inside.

"Ah, hell nawl. Do you need me to kick him out?" Gloria yells with her window done causing me to laugh.

"No, I got this."

"You sure because I got a baseball bat in my trunk."

"Go home G. I'll call if I need you."

I walk in to see Jacque asleep on the couch. I shake him.

"Um, hello. I thought you were supposed to get your things and leave, not fall asleep."

He yawns and looks at his watch. "I'm sorry, I just needed to close my eyes, for a moment and didn't realize it had gotten this late."

I turn to walk off but he grabs my hand, sitting up.

"Gwen, where do we go from here?"

"Jacque, you don't honestly think we'll stay together, do you?"

"I can change."

I sit next to him on the couch. "I don't want you to change for me but I want you to change for you and if being gay makes you happy, do you boo. Don't compromise your happiness for me because you'll only regret it."

"What about the baby?"

"I will never stop you from being a father and when I said I hadn't decided what I'm going to do, I lied because I'm keeping this baby. Is the current circumstances bad, yes but I believe God's timing is always perfect so I'm taking this as a blessing? You know, better than anybody, the struggles we've had getting pregnant and although we won't be married; it should not stop us from being great parents."

"I agree."

"I never thought I'd have the opportunity to carry a baby but—" I stop trying not to cry. If we have any chance on raising a baby with a healthy mental state, we cannot allow him or her to go through the same hell we have. Jacque, this must stop with us. We are both broken, by different circumstances and we run the risk of affecting a baby that hasn't even been born yet. I refuse to do that."

"What do we do?"

"We get our shit together, period! All the lying, living secret lives and this anger I have for my father, it must stop. Therefore, I've decided that I want more from myself and anybody around me because my now is sacred."

"What does that mean?" He asks.

"It means, if you can't add happiness, peace and love to my life and the life of this child; stay the hell away from us."

"Gwen, I am sorry for everything I've done and I know my apology doesn't take away your pain but I want you to know that I am."

"I hear you Jacque and I accept your apology."

"Thank you," I tell her, "but there's something else."

"Okay."

"I don't know if I'm ready to be a father."

"Are you serious?"

"I don't want to be like all the fathers I've seen. What if I turn out to be like Jimmy?"

"What if you don't?"

He looks defeated. "Will you give me some time?"

"Jacque, you can take all the time you need but we might not be here when you come back."

Jacque

I walk into the hotel room, letting the door close behind me before dropping my bags and keys and going straight to the wet bar. Taking out two bottles of liquor, I drink them both, replaying the conversation with Gwen.

I get upset and throw the small bottles into the wall. Exhausted and overwhelmed, I go back to the bar and drink until most of the bottles are empty. When I'm done, I fall back on the bed and cry myself to sleep.

I jump up when I feel the urge to vomit. I rush into the bathroom and barely make it to the toilet. After emptying the contents of my stomach, I slide into the floor.

Banging on the door

My eyes pop open and I realize I'm still on the floor. I try to pull myself up but my body weight is proving to be more of a hassle. Finally, up and sitting on the side of the bathtub, I am relieved when the banging stops. I touch my watch to see that it's after eight, in the morning.

I turn on the water for the shower, undress and step in, hoping the coldness shocks some sense into me. When I'm done, I clean off the mirror and the reflection of myself sickens me. My eyes are red and my face looks as if it has aged, twenty years.

With no immediate resolution, I brush my teeth and wash my face before wrapping a towel around my waist and opening the door.

"What the—Mark, what the hell are you doing in my room?"

"Oh my God, what happened to you?" He asks walking up and touching my face. "Did you get mugged or something."

I slap his hand away. "How did you get in my room?"

"I told the guy at the front desk I was your husband. You know I have a way of getting people to do what I want," he smiles.

"You need to get out of my room."

"What is wrong with you? I thought you'd be happy to see me."

"Why would you think that, when you're the reason I'm in this mess?"

"Baby—"

"Don't call me that!" I yell, causing him to step back.

"Why are you in such a mood?"

"Why am I in such a mood?" I restate the question. "Hmm, let's see. Maybe because I lost my freaking job, my wife and my reputation."

"Those are things that can be rectified sweetie. Now, come over here and let Mark take care of you. I'll make you forget all about what's her name."

"Her name is Gwen and you should know I told her who you are and everything Jimmy did to me growing up. She knows, I'm gay."

He drops his arms and his smile. "The world knows you're gay but why in the hell would you tell her anything about me?"

"BECAUSE I'M TIRED! Tired of all of this," I scream throwing my shirt across the room. "I'm tired of the lies, the secrets and I'm tired of this inner battle I'm having with myself."

"Nobody made you lie about who you are Jacque. You made the choice to stay in the closet boo but here's your chance to come out."

"Who are you to give advice when you're living a lie too?"

"Yea, well my wife is fine with our arrangement and if you would have married the girl, I told you too and not that mess you picked, we wouldn't be in this situation."

I look at him.

"Well, we wouldn't. Anyway, what's done is done. Get the divorce and move on."

"It's not that simple. We have a baby on the way."

"And? What does that have to do with me?"

"This isn't about you." I let out a deep breath, "just leave Mark because I need time to figure things out."

"What's there to figure out? I already told you that I am not about to be some gay dad, walking around with a man purse and pushing a stroller and neither are you. You must have forgotten that I've known you since you were eleven and intimately since sixteen?"

"How could I, when you won't let me forget?"

"Then it shouldn't be hard for you to remember that neither of us are father material. Hell, all you have to do is think about the role models we had."

"Is that why you wanted to ruin my life?"

"What are you talking about now?" He asks flinging his arms. "You've become so whiny these last few weeks. Hell, if I wanted to hear this, I'd stay home with Haley. Stop being a baby and give me a kiss."

I walk over to him and when he closes his eyes, I pick him up by his collar. His eyes pop open and he grabs my arm.

"Jacque," he fights, "stop!"

"Why, didn't you want my attention? Isn't it the reason you leaked the video that would ruin my career and my life?"

"I, I don't know what you're talking about," he stutters.

"You don't?" I shove him to the bed and grab my laptop. "When I got to my truck, after the embarrassment of being fired, walked out by security like a criminal while the internet watched me screw my boss; whose face was covered, I played this video over and over." I tell him, sitting on the bed. He scoots away. "I couldn't understand how someone could have recorded us without me noticing. Then I saw this." I fast forward the video then pause it, turning it around for him to see.

His eyes widen at the screen.

"See, even though your face is blurred, this is you looking directly into the camera. Now, common sense tells me, the only way you would have looked directly into the camera, you had to know it was there."

"That's not true."

I jump up and he puts his hands up in defense.

"Yes, okay, yes I recorded it but I didn't release it." He tries to grab my arm but I snatch away.

"You ruined my life. Why Mark? Why would you do this?"

"I'm sorry."

"That's not answering my question," I state.

"It was stupid but Haley was threatening to divorce me and I couldn't allow her to do that. I've worked hard to get where I am."

"And I didn't? I've had to work harder because of the color of my skin. Every time I apply for a promotion, I have to jump through hoops to prove I'm worthy of it, although my work should speak for itself. I've worked years trying to get promoted to VP and imagine my surprise when you waltz in and get it. Then, not even six months later, my job and reputation are both ruined because of you."

"I'm sorry Jacque," he says standing to fix his clothes. "Look, I love you and while I never meant for you to lose your job, it was either you or me. Unfortunately, it had to be you but you'll bounce back. You always do."

"I'll bounce back?" I repeat.

He walks over, touching my chest. "Baby, this doesn't have to be the end of your career. I know it looks like it but I've put in a few phone calls, with some friends, and they are willing to interview you but you'll have to move."

"Just like that, you've figured it all out."

"That's what I'm here for, to take care of you like always. Consider this, taking one for the team. Now, take a deep breath and let's talk about how I can help you relax."

I close my eyes and when I feel him touch the top of my pants, the anger takes over. I swing and connect with his face.

"Take one for the team. Is that what you said?" I ask, continuing to hit him. "That's all I've ever done." I swing again.

"Stop," he says over and over.

"That's it, little boy, take one for the team. Isn't that what your daddy and his friends would say, every time? Every time I'd cry after they'd make my jaws bleed from performing oral sex on him for hours or each time I'd have to miss two days of school from the rectal bleeding."

"Jacque, please—"

I hit him one last time before he stops moving.

Gwen

"Gwen, how are you feeling today?"

"I'm great Dr. Lea."

"That's good to hear. I know the nurse called you with your test results, do you have any questions about them before I start the exam?"

"No ma'am, I'm happy everything was normal."

She smiles. "Me too. What about your wrist?"

"I slammed a coffee cup down and a piece of it went through my wrist."

"Wow, how long ago?" She questions, beginning to remove the wrap.

"A few weeks ago."

"Let's take a look." She unwraps it. "It's healing nicely. The stitches will fully dissolve on their own, in another week or so but make sure you keep it dry and the bandage changed. If you happen to notice swelling, pus or you start running a fever; call me."

She cleans it, rewraps it and after the usual pre-natal checks, Dr. Lea helps me to sit up.

"Everything looks good and you're measuring on track for sixteen weeks. The next few weeks, you can expect a growth spurt as the baby's weight can sometimes double. We'll get an ultrasound today and if you'll like, you can find out the gender."

"Great. When will I begin to feel movement?"

"At about twenty weeks, they'll become more defined and frequent."

"Thank you, Dr. Lea."

"No problem. The nurse will take you to the ultrasound waiting area and if there's anything you need, don't hesitate to call the office."

Once I'm done there, I head to the office to get some work done. Getting out the car, I am met by a woman.

"Excuse me, are you Gwendolyn London."

"I am and you are?"

"My name is Haley Anton, Mark's wife."

"What can I do for you, Mrs. Anton?"

"You can start by telling me where my husband is."

I look around, "um, why in the hell would I know where your husband is? Isn't it your job to keep up with him?"

"Maybe if you kept your husband at home, I wouldn't be here."

I step a little closer to her because a client of Gloria's was walking out. "Wanch, I've had a long few weeks and I'm not in the right mindset to even entertain the foolishness of you. I haven't seen your husband and I, doggone sure, ain't looking for mine. May I suggest you do the same?"

I walk off before turning back to her, "and don't ever come to my job again. You may have more balls than your husband but the next time you think about coming for me, don't."

"I'm not scared of you. I ruined your husband's career and I can ruin yours too," she laughs. "Yea, I was the one who leaked the video."

"Oh, you must have thought that would keep your husband at home?" I laugh, "And yet, you're at my job looking for him. Girl, he doesn't want you, never has because all he's ever wanted is my husband."

She doesn't say anything.

"But you know this already, don't you?"

"I knew they grew up together and that's it."

"Oh sweetie, it's much more than that but you'll need to talk to your husband for the details."

"I would but he hasn't been home in three days and it's not like him. Can you at least call your husband?"

"And do what?"

"Ask if he's seen Mark. I'm just worried about my husband."

"Haley," I say walking closer to her. "Your husband is gay and probably laying on a beach somewhere with my husband. Let me ask you something? Do you have a house to stay in, car to drive and money in the bank?"

"Yes but—"

"Then go on about your life because it's apparent, he has. Good luck to you, though."

"Hey, who was that?" Gloria questions when I walk in.

"Mark's wife?"

"Girl, you lying! What did she want?"

"She's trying to find her husband."

"And she thought coming to you was the answer?"

"I guess so but I can care less about either of them," I tell her. "Anyway, guess what I have?" I hand her the ultrasound.

"Did you look?" She questions.

"No, I had them seal it because I know how excited you are to have a gender reveal."

She starts dancing.

"Bye Gloria. I want to get some work done before my appointment with Dr. Sharpe."

Restoration Session

I am sitting in the waiting area of the therapist office and my leg will not stop shaking.

"Here are a few forms I need you to fill out before you see the doctor," the receptionist says.

I spend ten minutes going through all the forms and when I'm done, I hand them to her to go over.

"Everything looks good," she says placing them on her desk. "You can follow me."

"Hi, you must be Gwendolyn London?"

"Yes, but please call me Gwen."

"It's nice to meet you, I'm Dr. Sharpe. Please have a seat."

We both sit.

"Before we begin, I like to start all sessions in prayer. Is that okay with you?"

"Yes, please."

She slides to the end of her chair and stretch her hands toward me.

"Dear God, as we come this afternoon petitioning your throne, we first say thank you for another day. God, as we gather in your presence, I ask for your will to be done. Fasten Gwen with the strength to open the dark places so that they can be filled with light. Give her hope to know whatever was broken before, can now be healed by you. In the matchless name of Jesus, amen."

"Amen," I repeat sliding back into my chair as she grabs her computer tablet.

"Tell me how you came to be here today."

"My pastor recommended your colleague, Dr. Mitchell but I know she wasn't accepting any new clients. The young lady, I spoke too when I made the appointment told me about you."

"Would you rather wait and speak to Dr. Mitchell because I can transfer you to her, if you'd like?" She inquires.

"Oh no, that's not necessary. I'm fine with you."

She nods. "Tell me about you Gwen."

"Well, my full name is Gwendolyn London. I am born and raised in Memphis. My mother is still living and I have an older sister, Gloria. I've been married for six years, pregnant with my first baby and I'm into real estate. Until recently, I thought my life was good."

"What happened to change your thinking?"

"I found out my husband was having an affair," I pause, "with a man."

"How did that make you feel?"

"You all really ask that question?"

"Yes, and I know it seems silly but we ask it, in order to gauge your emotional state."

"I see. Well, it made me feel like shit. Excuse my language."

"Is that because he cheated or more because he cheated with a man?"

"The fact that he cheated and didn't have the courage to be honest with me." I answer.

"Did you know of your husband's desire to be with men?"

"God no and had someone told me he was gay; I would have argued them up and down because I never saw the signs."

"Does that make you feel guilty about his actions?"

"No."

"Good, because the truth is Gwen, sometimes there aren't any signs. Especially when people are great at suppressing their urges. Tell me how you met your husband."

"It was twelve years ago, while I was at a real estate conference in Washington. He was in the city, for his job and we started talking and that's when I learned he was from Memphis, too. At the time, I was in 'F' all men mode and wasn't looking for a relationship."

"Why is that?" She inquires while taking notes.

"I'd spent years trying to replace the love I lacked from my daddy. He left when I was twelve, for my mom's best friend, who happened to be married to his best friend; and replaced us with a whole new family. I was devastated and lost because I was a daddy's girl and I couldn't understand why he'd abandoned us. It was like, he was there one minute and gone the next."

"How did you handle losing that relationship?"

"I began sleeping, well not really sleeping, but having sex with anything that had a hard penis and a mouth capable of making me promises. The crazy part, I knew they were lying but I accepted whatever and God forbid when they lied or hurt me. I didn't care about going to jail after busting out windows, slashing tires, bleaching clothes and everything else. I'd even destroy an apartment. It didn't matter. If they hurt me, I made sure to hurt them back."

I pause but she doesn't say anything.

"Then I met Calvin."

"Who's he?"

"He was a smooth talker and if that man said we were going to the moon, my stupid tail would have packed a bag and followed him. I was gullible, he knew it and took full advantage of it. He was good, though," I chuckle. "Good in the sense of an actor because he played his part well. He would buy me whatever I wanted, hold me the nights I craved it, took me on the fancy vacations and gave me unlimited access to him. What I didn't realize, he was softening me up."

"For what?"

"To accept whatever else he wanted me to do. After we'd been dating for six months, he started having these poker parties. My foolish self was right there, with my head in the clouds while he was putting me up as collateral. When he lost, he lost big and he knew he could talk me into doing whatever, for him. The whatever, was using my body to pay off his debts."

"Did you stop it?"

"Nope," I wipe the tears that wouldn't stop, "If it meant he was happy, I did it because I thought his happiness was my happiness but I was wrong. His happiness caused me hell but I couldn't see it because I was too blinded by my quest to fill the void, in my heart. I definitely didn't stop it because then I'd lose him."

"Was he ever abusive?"

"Had you asked me that, a few years ago, I would have said no but it was a form of physical abuse; just with no bruises? Oh, and control. He could control me even if he was out of the state. He'd call and tell me, who was coming over and what I needed to wear to make sure they were happy. Man, I was a fool."

"You were foolish, not a fool."

"Is there a difference?" I question.

"A fool is a noun or a person who acts unwisely but foolish is an adjective to describe the actions of the person. Gwen, you can be foolish without being a fool. When Job told his wife, in Job two and ten, you speak as one of the foolish women, he was referring to her actions to the situation they were being faced with. Your actions were foolish because, you too, were responding to what you saw and received."

"I should have known better, though."

"How? Who taught you? Have you read books on how not to be foolish or gullible for a man? Have you been to the classes? Beloved, you aren't the first woman who's been foolish over a man and you will not be the last. However, to ensure you never go there again, you have to deal with the underlying issues of what broke you in the first place."

"You're right," I reply.

"How did you finally get away from him?"

"After about a year, he dumped me and moved on to somebody whose body wasn't as used."

"Leaving you broken," Dr. Sharpe says.

"Leaving me more broken," I correct. "But I did what I did best, tore up everything I possibly could of his and moved to another bad relationship. Then, I got tired."

"What made you tired then that didn't before?"

"My reflection. I was tired of looking at myself in the mirror because I'd started hating who I'd become and I knew if I didn't make a change, I'd eventually kill myself."

"Did you ever tell anybody?" She questions.

"Not at first, not even my sister because I was ashamed at what I'd allowed myself to become. I gave pieces of my heart to anybody who acted like they wanted it and by the time I woke up from the coma of low self-esteem and self-inflicted wounds, there were only a few salvageable pieces left." I smile through my tears. "So, I locked those babies up and vowed to never give my heart to another man and I spent the next years of my life, finding me."

"But you got married. What was different about him?"

"Jacque came correct." I laugh, still wiping tears. "He wanted to know me, not my body and when I told him about my past, he didn't judge me or run. Dr. Sharpe, me and that man would stay on the phone for hours and we enjoyed each other's company. He could tell when I was having a bad day, by the sound of my voice. He'd even buy my favorite things, when it was that time of the month because he knew I was in pain.

He was in the last year of his Master's program and I often talked about getting my real estate license. One night, I came home and he had all the books and resources I needed to get the ball rolling. He was the one who pushed me and when I didn't think I was going to make it, he prayed with me. I'd never had a man pray for me."

"He covered you," she says. "Nevertheless, he was only doing the same thing the others had done, in your past, just in a different way."

"What do you mean?"

"He made you feel whole and safe by pretending to fill what you thought was missing and you missed it because it was wrapped differently. Truth is, Gwen, you were both broken pieces, drawn to one another by your inward need. You wanted love and he, more than likely, needed validation."

"Wow. I never thought of that but it all makes sense and I missed it."

"It wasn't time for you to see it but God reveals all things, when we're ready," she says looking at her watch. "That's our time for today. If you'd like to make another appointment, you can do so with Ingrid before you leave."

"I will. Thank you, Dr. Sharpe."

"You're welcome. Let's pray."

We stand.

"Father, we thank you for this new path of restoration. Now, God, don't allow Gwen to be discouraged or rocked by the waves of her storm. Guide her back to you and let her rest in the comforts of your arms. And as we leave here, allow our journey to be safe and her minds to be at ease. Give her strength to continue this journey and find the process to put together the pieces of her that are broken. We thank you God. Amen."

Gwen

I roll over, when I hear my phone vibrating. "Hello, what, who is this? You're where? You've got to be kidding me? Fine, I'm on the way."

I stretch out on my back, first trying to make sure I heard what I heard and second, to come to terms with it being four in the morning.

Letting out an agitated breath, I throw the covers back and get up.

After spending three hours at a bail bondsman and three more hours sitting outside of the Memphis Jail, Jacque was finally being released. The tap on the window causes my eyes to pop open.

Yawning, I hit the button to unlock the doors. He gets in and I look upside his head. When I part my lips, he holds up his hand.

"Please Gwen, I know this looks bad but I'll explain everything after a shower and nap."

"That's fine but you stink," I tell him letting the window down.

Once Jacque and I, make it to the house, after getting his things from the hotel, he showers and falls asleep in the guestroom. He's been out for a while so I cooked dinner while getting some work done.

He explained getting arrested, a few days ago, for beating Mark. He hadn't called because he was embarrassed and thought he could wait it out. When the conditions got to him, he tried calling his lawyer but he was away, dealing with an emergency family thing and he had no choice but to call me.

When the doorbell rings, I pause the TV to open the door for Gloria, who's dropping off some papers I need to sign. Instead, I am shocked by the person standing on my porch.

"Um, can I help you?"

"Gwen, I know I have no right to be here but I really need to talk to you."

"Who gave you my address?"

"Your mother but don't be mad at her, she knows I'm in a desperate situation."

"Look David, I don't care how desperate you are but coming here will not change my mind. I'm not pretending to be some happy family so you can shine in the limelight. So, goodbye."

"Gwen, please. I don't need you to say anything good but don't say nothing at all."

I chuckle, "dude get off my porch."

"Will you hear me out?" He asks putting his hand on the door.

"Why? Nothing you say or do, at this point matters to me or my life. As a matter-of-fact, take two steps back and allow me to close the door, on you, the same way you did to me. Then you'll know how I felt when I showed up at your house and you ignored me. Do you remember that, dad?"

"Yes, and I'm sorry. There are a lot of things I did wrong and walking out on you and your sister is at the top of that list." He somberly says.

"No, you didn't only walk out. You walked out, erased any footprints and made damn sure we couldn't find you again. You made a choice and now I'm making one, show yourself out of my house."

"I'm sorry."

I turn back to face him. "Yea, well so am I. I am sorry to have your DNA running through my veins. Do you know how broken you left me? HUH," I yell? "You broke me so bad that I was willing to give any man, who crossed my path, a piece of me because I couldn't understand what I did to make you hate me so much. All I ever wanted was my daddy's love and you didn't care.

That day, at your house, I was humiliated. I sat on your porch, crying for you and you ignored me. When I left there, in the car, I'd just purchased with my savings, I drove down to the Mississippi River and I contemplated driving it in. You want to know why? Because I didn't want to go on living with this brokenness."

"Sister," Gloria says, with tears streaming down her face. I hadn't even realized she'd come in. "You never told me that."

I cry. "There's a lot of things, in my past, I haven't told you because I was too ashamed at what I allowed him to turn me into. However, while I'm confessing dad, you ought to know that I hated myself. For a long time, I hated me and because I did, I willingly gave myself away to men. Calvin, though," I chuckle, "he was the worst. He sold me to his friends, for sex, and I let him because I thought he loved me."

"Sister, you don't have to do this." She says, walking towards me.

"No Gloria, he needs to know what he did. He broke my heart before any other man could, so he needs to know. You see, daddy, all I ever wanted was to feel loved and accepted but truth is, I was still that rejected girl, standing on her daddy's porch and no matter how many men I slept with, it couldn't repair it."

They both stare at me.

"I prayed, many nights, for God to stop my heart because I didn't have the courage to take my life. I wanted too, oh, the pain was just that bad but He wouldn't let me die."

"Gwen, that's enough." Gloria say walking closer to me. "David, you need to leave."

"Wait," David says. "Gwen and Gloria, no amount of words will be able to make up for the way I treated you girls or your mom. I was selfish and lowdown but I've asked God to forgive me. Now, I'm asking you to forgive me too. Don't let me be the reason you don't find the love you need to sustain you in this life. Don't allow your hatred for me to be the reason you stay in this dark place. I'll have to atone for my sins and I will but don't follow in my footsteps. You have an opportunity to break the curse."

"Aw," Gloria says. "The Bishop is preaching. Well, save it for your congregation because your words don't mean shit to us."

I walk over and give him a half hug.

"I forgive you, not for you but for me and I pray God has mercy on your soul."

Gloria looks at him, "yeah, I ain't there yet."

"I love you girls and I truly am sorry."

He turns to walk out when Jacque comes down the hall.

"Wayne?"

Jacque

"What did you call him?" Gwen asks.

"What in the hell are you doing in my house?" I ask through clenched teeth, ignoring Gwen. "How did you find me?"

Gloria steps up, "Who in the hell is Wayne?"

"Jocky," David says looking from me to them, with his eyes lighting up.

"Don't call me that."

"This doesn't make sense," Gwen tries to rectify. "How do you know my father?"

"Your father," I state, stumbling back. "This man is your father?"

"Yes, how do you know him?"

"He's one of the men who raped me."

"Wait, he's the friend of the step-daddy that—oh hell nawl!" Gloria hollers at David.

"I don't know what he told you but he's lying," David yells.

"You were friends with my stepdad, Jimmy. You and he, along with Mr. Anton would take us on camping trips. Me, Mark and Bart."

"But he doesn't have a son," Gwen says.

"Marjorie did," Gloria adds. "Bart was Marjorie's son, from her first marriage," she says trying to remember. "He killed himself by jumping from the roof of his dorm. It was all over the news."

"Did you know who I was when we met?" Gwen asks me.

"Of course not. I had no idea this bastard was your father. The last time I saw him, I was twenty. He showed up at our house and," I stopped. "Anyway, I moved away from my mom, stepdad and him because

I knew with the anger, building in me, I'd end up killing one of them."

"Oh my God, I'm going to be sick." Gwen runs to the bathroom with Gloria behind her.

"Jock—I mean Jacque, how have you been?"

"None of your damn business. Now, get out of my house."

"Look, I didn't come here for you. I didn't even know who my daughter was married too."

"Then why are you here?"

"I'm being vetted by the board of the National Baptist Convention and I don't need my daughters spewing anything negative about me. I only came to talk to them but since you're here, you need to keep your mouth closed too."

"And if I don't?"

"Please don't make me show you how far my hand can reach. Boy, there's been ample times I could have gotten to you. While you were in college at Austin Peay University or when you did that intern—"

"I'm not afraid of you."

"You should be because I'd hate for anything to happen to you, while your wife is pregnant. Then I'd have to look after your child, you know, once you're gone and God, I hope it's a boy. I'm sure he'll enjoy the camping trips as much as you did."

I grab him and push him against the wall.

"I'm not that scared little boy whose life you ruined, all those years ago. Today, I'm a man who has a family to protect and if you ever come near me or my wife again, I'll do what I should have done a long time ago and blow your got-damn brains out."

I let him go and he coughs, to catch his breath then he laughs. He stands up straight. "You do have a mean fist. Should I be scared that you're going to beat me like you did Mark?"

I look at him.

"Oh, Mark didn't tell you that we're still in contact? Yea, he still loves old Wayne. Who do you think got him the job—as your boss?" He laughs.

"You filthy, vile, rickety and good for nothing child molester, it's time for you to go!" Gloria says coming into the living room.

"You've always have had a disrespectful mouth and the only reason I never put you in your place is because of your mother. She should have sent your ass to Job Corp, like I told her too. Maybe then you would have gotten a taste for boys." He laughs again, reaching to rub her face. She steps back, picks up a vase and hits him in the mouth. He doubles over as blood spills onto the floor.

"Nigga, the only one who needs to be put any place, is you in a grave," she says dropping the pieces of vase left in her hands before spitting on him.

I grab him, again and drag him to the door. Once it's open, I throw him off the porch and into the grass.

"What are you doing to my husband?" A lady screams, getting out the car.

"Throwing out the trash. Get him off my property and don't ever come back here." I go back into the house, slam the door and encounter Gwen's hand, slapping me across the face.

She cries. "Did you know who I was, this entire time, did you know?"

"No, I promise I had no idea who you were. I didn't even know he was your father because Jimmy said he lived in Oklahoma and you were born and raised here. Whenever you mentioned him, you said David and I only knew him as Wayne."

"His name is David Wayne Page and he moved there after he and my mom divorced. But how could you not know? This man has been all over the TV?"

"I still wouldn't have put it together that he was your father. Gwen, you only talked about your dad, when we first met. Even then, you didn't have pictures of him, not even at your mom's house." I move closer to her. "Gwen, do you honestly think I chose you because of your father? That man is as evil as they come. I only wish I'd killed him and Jimmy, all those years ago. Babe, please say you believe me. I love you."

"No, don't touch me," she snaps. "You're just like him."

"I'm not a child molester!"

"No, you're a liar. I guess I can give you credit for sticking around but we both know you don't love me. Hell, you don't even love yourself. Nonetheless, it's my fault because I let my guard down. Not anymore, though because I'm done being used and I'm damn sure done being broken."

"I'm just as broken as you are. Don't you see that? I didn't ask for any of this. I didn't ask to be molested and violated, over and over. I didn't ask for this!"

"That's not my problem anymore."

"Why is it, you can be broken and get grace but I can't? Isn't that a double standard?"

"Oh, now you know the Bible? Dude, I couldn't even get you to go to church and now you want me to feel guilty about not giving you grace?"

"Gwen, I hated everything about church because it reminded me of Wayne, Jimmy and Mark Sr. They acted like these Godly man when they were nothing but devils. My step father would preach and lay hands on folks then turn right around and touch me, inappropriately. Yes, I know I've messed up and I'm finally admitting I need help. I'm broken too."

"You're right, we are both broken but the difference is, I told you of my past and you should have done the same."

"I couldn't!"

"YES YOU COULD! Twelve years ago, when I was pouring my heart out to you, you should have been honest and gave me the option of staying. The same choice I gave you but you didn't. Instead, you allowed me to give myself to you, fall in love and now I'm carrying a baby who is already bound to brokenness and it hasn't even taken its first breath in the world. And for the record, I don't owe you grace, God does. I need some air. Please don't be here when I get back."

"Gwen wait," I say to her as she grabs her purse and leaves.

Gwen

"Gwen, wait," Gloria calls following behind me as I walk out into the garage.

"G, I need to get out of here."

"Then I'm coming with you but let me drive because you drive too fast when you're mad."

She's right so we switch seats.

"Where to?"

I look at her and she nods.

We make the thirty-minute drive to my mother's house. When she opens the door, we barge in.

"Did you know?" I ask with venom in my voice.

"Know what?"

"Did you know our father was a child molester?"

Her hand drops from the door knob.

"Wow," Gloria says. "You knew this entire time and you did nothing to stop him?"

"I didn't know for sure but I'd heard the rumors."

"Why didn't you do something?"

"I let him leave, didn't I? You should be thankful, he liked little boys and not girls."

"You're just as sick as he is. Damn," I tell her. "Our entire bloodline is damaged."

"Girl, ain't nobody damaged in this family but your sick ass daddy."

"AND YOU!" I scream. "You're just as sick as he is for doing nothing to stop him."

"What was I supposed to do? Warn the bitch he left me for? I think not. She wanted him and she got him with all his demons."

"Yea but Jacque got him too," Gloria tells her.

"What? What does Jacque have to do with this?"

"David molested him."

"Well, how was I supposed to know that? David left and the last time I saw him was on your thirteenth birthday. So, whatever happened to Jacque, I had nothing to do with. Your father moved on and I did too."

"Jacque's blood is on your hands, mother because you knew David was a monster and did nothing. Instead of turning him in to the police, you turned him loose on the streets of Memphis and wherever else. Do you know how many lives he's ruined?" Gloria ask her.

"Look, I will not stand here and let you two disrespect me. David was a grown man and the only ones I had a responsibility to protect was you and Gloria. I did that."

"What about the baby who's growing inside of me?" I ask, as tears fall. "How am I supposed to compete with demons that have been attached to our bloodline since before we were born? How am I supposed to protect my child from becoming subject to these same curses?"

"You do what I did? Pray you don't have a boy," she somberly replies.

"You're a piece of work," Gloria says facing her, "and I pray you never get what you deserve. Sister, let's go."

We get in the car and Gloria starts to drive.

"I can't have this baby," I blurt.

"Gwendolyn Javon London Page, I will slap fire from you if you even think about harming my nephew."

"It's a boy?"

"Shit! See what you made me do."

I cry harder and she pulls over.

"Gwen, give me your hand and look at me. This baby you're carrying shall not bear the weight of our bloodline because we have the power to destroy it. If anything, knowing it is a boy should give you more determination to open your mouth and decree it so. I refuse to sit by, like mother did and watch it continue. If I have to buy a batch of holy oil, a case of prayer clothes and spend every free minute on the altar; I'll do it. My nephew will not be subject to this. Do you hear me?"

I shake my head, yes.

"Good."

She releases me and it's then we notice flashing lights behind us.

A knock on the window, causes us both to jump. Gloria turns to let it down.

"Are you ladies okay," the police officer asks, flashing the light into the car. "I saw you pull over."

"Yes, my sister was having a moment and I needed to pull over and calm her down."

"Would you like me to call for an ambulance?"

"Oh no, that's not necessary. We were actually getting ready to leave." Gloria responds looking up. "Nikki?"

The officer bends down. "G? Girl, I didn't realize it was you. How have you been?"

She opens the door and gets out, leaving it cracked. After they give each other a hug, Gloria gets back in.

"I didn't know you were with the Memphis Police Department. The last time we talked it was, what—"

"Five years ago," she finishes. "I was moving out of state with my wife but I'm divorced now and been back for, almost two years."

"Well, we definitely need to catch up, over drinks."

"Sounds good to me. Here," she hands her phone through the window, "put your number in and I'll call you tonight when I'm off."

When she's done, she rolls the window up and I'm looking at her.

"What? She's just an old friend."

"If you say so."

Jacque

I walk into High Point Christian Center. I hadn't told Gwen I was coming because we haven't been communicating, lately but this morning, I felt the need to come.

"Welcome to High Point," the usher says giving me a tithing envelope and a program. "Enjoy the service."

I find a seat, close to the back as worship begins. The choir stands and begins to sing an old song by Kirk Franklin, one I hadn't heard in years. It's called Savior, more than life to me.

I close my eyes as they sing.

"Savior, more than life to me. You are the joy and air I breathe, no other lover shall there be that makes my spirit say. Hold me close don't let me go, you're the only friend I'll ever know that is why I love you so. More than life to me. You're more than life to me."

It has been years since I've stepped foot inside a church, for worship and the tugging in my spirit was reminding me of it. The leader joins and the choir continues to sing.

"More, Lord you're more. I've been searchin' and you are more, more, more. Yes, you are, you are more than life to me. Yes, you are and that is why I love you so. More than life to me."

As the program flows, it's time for the pastor to preach.

"This morning, our reading will come from Jeremiah eighteen, verses one through ten." Pastor Magnolia Reeves says, at the podium. "It reads, *'The Lord gave another message to Jeremiah. He said, go down to the potter's shop, and I will speak to you there. So, I did as he told me and found the potter working at his wheel. But the jar he was making did not turn out as he had hoped, so he crushed it into a lump of clay again and started over.'* Amen."

"Amen," the congregation says.

"If I had to give a title to this text, it'd be, a reusable mess. Say, a reusable mess."

"Reusable mess," the congregation repeats.

"In this passage of scripture, Jeremiah is instructed to go down to the potter's shop. When he gets there, it just happens to be at the same time the potter is working with a lump of clay. Jeremiah watches the potter and as he works it, the Bible says, it doesn't turn out like the potter wants but instead of throwing the clay out, he simply takes it off the wheel, rolls it back into a lump and starts again.

What am I getting at? You, beloved, are like this lump of clay that God is molding and shaping. Sometimes, we mess up because we're in a natural world surrounded by sin and temptations. When we do mess up, God doesn't discard us, throwing us away from Him like man. Instead, He takes us, the lump of clay and begins to smooth out our rough and broken pieces. He places us on the wheel and begins to patch up the breaks He didn't intend to be there.

Why? Because we're a reusable mess. Isaiah sixty-four and eight says, *'and yet, O LORD, you are our Father. We are the clay, and you are the potter. We all are formed by your hand.'* People of God, we are the clay and we're, every day, being molded by God which means, we are a reusable mess. You can sit there and act like you aren't but if you were to think about some of the stuff you've been in and came out of; you'd declare, I'm a mess too. But aren't you glad, God doesn't cast us out?

Every time we mess up, we get a blemish in our clay. Every time we lie on somebody, we get a blemish in our clay. Every time we misuse folk, we get a blemish in our clay. Each time we back slide, we get a blemish in our clay. The times when we covet or wish for other folk's blessings, we get a blemish in our clay. Every time we doubt God, we get a blemish in our clay. Every time we sin, and every time we come into God's house and act like He hasn't done anything for us, we get a blemish in our clay. Every time we get the audacity to treat God like He isn't worthy, we get a blemish in our clay.

Oh, but guess what? Lean in child of God because I need you to get this. Even after all the stuff we've done, did or will do; God doesn't take His hand from us. At our dirtiest, God still has His foot on the pedal and us on the well, purposefully molding us into what He has desired us to be. God, daily, continues to work the mess out of our clay. He simply reshapes us, the clay, back into the usable vessel He knows we can be. Each time we repent and come back to Him, God is molding the mess out of our clay because we are a reusable mess!"

"Yes God, amen," the congregation shouts.

She finishes her sermon and opens the altar.

"Don't allow people to make you feel bad for pleading guilty, admitting your faults and wanting help, when they are just as damaged but choosing to be a fugitive instead of free. People of God, your childhood problems don't go away just because you've grown up. Your adult problems are those same problems and they didn't get healed, they simply aged. But how many of you know, God's blood has the power to wash up clean? You may be a mess but you have the opportunity now, to give yourself to a God who will reshape us. Are you willing?"

It seems like she's talking directly to me and before I can stop myself, I'm walking to the altar.

Gwen

"Girl, I must be seeing things," Gloria says elbowing me.

"What?"

"Look," she nods.

I turn in the direction she's looking and my mouth falls open. On the altar is Jacque.

"Well, aren't you going to go up there?"

Tears are forming in my eyes. "Nope, this is something he needs to do for himself."

After church, I try to find Jacque but he's gone. I call him and he doesn't answer. Gloria and I stop to eat before going our separate ways. She has a date with Nikki later and I'm happy she's taking control of her life.

Inside the car, my phone rings with a call from Jacque. I put the car in park and connect the Bluetooth.

"Hey, you called?" He questions.

"Yeah, I was trying to catch you before you left church. Why didn't you tell me you were coming?"

"To be honest, I didn't know I was. Babe, it's been so long since I've gone to church for something other than a funeral."

"I know," I chuckle, "because I remember the fights, we used to have on Sunday morning. I never knew they were because of David."

"I can't blame him anymore because I should have gotten to know God for myself instead of allowing him to taint my understanding of who He is. I have to admit, your pastor is very good."

"I know, she's amazing. I would have liked for you to meet her."

"Maybe I will, when I visit again but there's something, I need to talk to you about."

"Please don't let it be any more bad news."

"I've been offered a job," he pauses, "in Houston."

"Houston? Wow, I didn't know you'd applied for any out of state jobs."

"I had no choice. Since that video was leaked, I haven't been able to find anything in the city and I think the change will do me good."

"What about the charges you have pending for assault?"

"I'm hoping they will be dropped when I go to court on Friday."

"Have you talked to Mark?"

"No and I hope it stays that way," he says.

"What about David?"

"Yes, he called me and wanted to meet. I declined then he sends me an email and I deleted it without reading it. I just don't understand how he can even feel comfortable contacting me, after all these years."

"Have you thought about speaking out, against him?"

"I did, before, but he's a big time Bishop and I'm just a guy with a gay sex tape that has gone viral. I don't know if I even want the headache or the added attention. Plus, I remember what happened the last time I spoke out."

"You were a child then but now, you're an adult and you can use your voice, even if it's making a post on social media. People need to know who the real David Page is because if he hurt you and your friends, all those years ago; he hasn't stopped."

"I'll think about it, once I'm settled in Houston."

"Jacque, although things between us, did not work out and a little strained, I do want you to be happy and I apologize for some of the things I said the other night. I was angry and confused."

"I know and I apologize for everything too because had I been honest, before, we wouldn't be in this situation. I kept quiet because I was asking myself, but is there love worth fighting for and my flesh was saying yes but in my heart; I knew it was time to let you go."

"Sometimes leaving is easier," I say, "because it keeps us from having to admit our flaws and owning up to our mistakes. Although, I don't know how we move on from this, one thing is for sure, I got to move on because I can't keep harboring this anger."

He sighs.

"I know," I laugh. "I have an idea and this may sound crazy but why don't you join me at my counseling session tomorrow."

"Are you sure?"

"Yes. You're about to move to Houston, to start over and we have to co-exist for the sake of this baby. It won't be a magic eraser for our problems but it can be a start."

"Okay. Send me the address and time and I'll be there."

I hang up and text him the information. I don't know if it's the best thing but it can't hurt.

Restoration Session

Dr. Sharpe

"Good afternoon Gwen, are you ready?" I ask from the door of my office.

"I am but I'm waiting on my husband. I hope you don't mind that I've invited him to this session." She replies, following me into the office.

"Not as long as you're okay with it."

"I think I am," she says before sitting down.

"You think?"

"Dr. Sharpe, I'm just tired of the fighting and if this helps us exist, in the same space then I'm willing."

"I'm sorry for being late," Jacque says rushing in, "but I got caught in traffic."

"You must be Jacque," I say standing to greet him.

"I am and it's nice to meet you."

"Please come in. My name is Dr. Sharpe and I like to begin all sessions in prayer, is that okay with you Jacque?"

"Sure."

"Then, let's pray. Dear God, we take this moment to pause in thanksgiving to you. Thank you for another day and for the strength of this man and woman you've allowed to come, looking for peace and understanding. God, I ask you to guide this restoration session so that hope and joy may be restored. Speak through your servant so that I may work by the power you've given. Open the eyes, ears and mind of Gwen and Jacque that they may find their joy again, by leaning on you and not their understanding. In your name, Jesus, we pray, amen."

"Amen."

"Gwen, I'll start with you. How are you today?"

"I'm okay, I guess or shall I say I'm getting better. Taking it a day at a time but I'm better than I was before."

"That's good and Jacque, what about you?"

"To be honest, these last few months have been a struggle and—"

"And what? This is a safe place, Jacque and here you can express yourself without judgement. Go ahead."

He sits up. "These last few months have been a struggle and a few times, I've thought about ending my life."

He looks over at Gwen, again.

"Gwen, how does that make you feel to hear that?"

"He's not by himself, Dr. Sharpe. When I, unintentionally, cut my wrist, I begged my sister to let me bleed to death because I didn't think I could live with anymore pain. I didn't care about anything or anybody, all I wanted was for the pain to stop."

"I'm sorry," Jacque whispers.

"What did you say Jacque?"

"I was apologizing to Gwen."

"Why?" I question.

"I'm the reason she's feeling this way."

"Is that true Gwen? Is your husband the reason?"

"Partly but he isn't the only reason. I've dealt with so much rejection, in my life and finding out he was cheating, bought all those suppressed memories back to the surface. Recently, I found out he was molested by my father and that my sister is gay. So, it's not all on him because I was broken long before him. In a way, I think he was trying to help me heal but he couldn't because he was broken too. I realize now, Dr. Sharpe, he wasn't the person to heal me, God and therapy is. Therefore, I want him to stop apologizing."

"Tell him," I instruct.

She turns to Jacque. "Please stop apologizing. I know you messed up and I also know you're sorry for it but it doesn't change what you did. Nonetheless, I accept your apology and I forgive you. All I want is for us to heal and be happy."

"Thank you," he says, "but I need you to know that I never meant to hurt you. I realize, now, I wasn't ready to be a husband but it felt good to be needed by you. You made me feel like a man, Gwen and although I'd work hard to be manly, with the tattoos and suits; inwardly, I felt like a fraud."

"Why is that Jacque?" I question.

"That's what I was. I was pretending to be the perfect husband and I think I was good at it but I was failing me. Pastor Reeves said something, at church yesterday that really solidified everything for me. She said, your childhood problems don't go away just because you've grown up. Your adult problems are those same problems and they didn't get healed, they simply aged."

"Amen," I laugh.

"She was right," Dr. Sharpe says. "We think just because we've pushed our issues down or don't talk about them, they'll go away but they don't. They are like seeds that have blossomed into plants. Some seasons, plants that once bloomed will look dead or dormant but as soon as the season changes, they spring back up. Childhood traumas, unhealed wounds and soul ties can be just like those dormant plants.

Unlike plants, they don't have to wait until the season changes because they can pop up at the most in opportune time, wreaking havoc. Therefore, we must deal with it by digging up what doesn't belong and cutting off what has the potential to hurt us. It's easy to plant but hard to prune."

"What do we do now, Dr. Sharpe?"

"You make the decision on what you want to do with the bad seeds that are inside of you. Either you can keep them buried, giving them permission to sprout, when they want or you can pluck them up and replant something new. Here's the thing, both takes work and it's going to hurt. However, it gives you the opportunity to now grow something beneficial and not burdensome. Be willing to change, be willing to get help and be willing to be you. No matter how hard it gets."

They look at each other.

"Gwen, take Jacque's hand," I direct her. "Now, tell him it's okay to be who he is."

"Jacque London, I've loved you for the last twelve years of my life. You helped me grow into the person I am today. You looked passed everything I did, you helped to clean up the messes I made and you gave me the freedom to be me. Today, I'm giving you back your freedom along with my blessing to be you."

He lowers his head as the tears fall. Gwen touches his chin to lift his head. "You are free now." She pulls him into a hug and he begins to cry, finally releasing all the emotions he's had pinned up.

I walk over and put my hand on both of their backs.

"Our Father in Heaven, I come before you with a spirit of thanksgiving. Thank you, God for your son and daughter, whom my hands are touching. God, you are aware of everything they've had to deal with and now I ask you to deliver them. God, by your power, pluck up whatever needs to be plucked up and prune away any and everybody that means them no good. Father, while you're pruning and taking away, restore.

Restore light into the dark places, restore hope into the hardened areas and restore strength where it belongs. God and while you're working, grant them the freedom to walk in the shoes of who you've called them to be. Release them from the prison of pain, the barrel of brokenness and the repositories of rejection.

God, grant them clemency to conquer what has tried to kill them.

Give Gwen her glory and give Jacque back his joy. For they are your children, you made them, you shaped them and you molded them. That is why, I know you didn't create them to suffer all the days of their life. So, I'll count their suffering, in this season, as finished and I'll bid it goodbye, for now and from this day forward, there shall be peace. Peace to sleep and peace to live. We love you Lord and we seal this prayer with amen."

Jacque

It's been about two months since everything happened. I've moved to Houston but it hasn't stopped me from having nightmares of those camping trips. Most nights, I'm up staring at the ceiling. I haven't heard from Wayne/David but Mark has been calling, texting and emailing; nonstop.

I mistakenly answered a call from another number, the other night and it was him. He was going on and on about me owing him for getting the charges, against me, dropped. He wanted to come here and when I declined, he began screaming to the top of his lungs. I had to eventually hang up and add that number to the block list too.

The sad part of it, I felt bad about blocking him because Mark and I have known each other since we were eleven. He was the one who was there for me, the nights Jimmy would beat me. He was the one who would give me a place to sleep, when I'd run away. It has always been Mark and I think, in some way, we developed a bond over our brokenness. It never mattered that years would put distance between us because it couldn't stop us from being emotionally connected.

Nonetheless, it was very unhealthy for the both of us.

When he married Haley, I thought it would be what he needed to finally let me go but it didn't. Truth is, it made it worse because Haley gave him the freedom to be him, if he kept her happy. He tried to set me up with one of Haley's friends but she didn't compare to Gwen.

Meeting Gwen changed me.

Well, that's the lie I told myself because honestly, all it changed me into was a person who could hide his flaws. Recently, I've come to terms with knowing, Gwen and I wasn't good for each other. She was only filling a void, the same as what I was doing for her. We were both broken pieces that didn't fit, no matter how we tried but we made it look good.

Beautiful, broken pieces.

Anyway, I've had to block numerous random numbers, because Mark knew I couldn't change my number; being in the midst of applying for jobs. However, now that I'm working and here in Houston, TX, I will be changing it, first thing in the morning.

At this moment, though, I am staring at my laptop. Dr. Sharpe referred me to a local therapist, who has been great in helping me overcome my issues and tonight, she gave me an assignment.

FACE YOUR FEARS.

I open Facebook and stare at the box, 'What's on your mind, Jacque?' I almost grab a bottle of whiskey, for a few shots but I decide against it because what I'm about to share needs to be from a level head.

I close my eyes, take a deep breath, open them and begin to type.

Facebook Post | December 12, 2018

#longpostalert Suicide is defined as intentionally taking your own life but it's so much more than this definition. Suicide isn't a diagnosis, a prescription can prevent neither is it a rash some magical cream can resolve. It's a serious epidemic that is becoming all too serious and I know because I've been there.

You may see the pictures I post, the statuses I share but truth is, I'm broken and I have been for a long time. (Insert sigh.) The pictures, I have the strength to show, are the days my depression isn't as bad or my nightmares didn't keep me up. The smiles are the days the voices are silent. Good days, are few and far between yet nobody knows because I've become good at faking it.

My wife, she has been there but even she didn't know how broken I was because I'm a great pretender. Nonetheless, I realize I couldn't be for her what she needed because I didn't know how to be who I was. Reality is, I'm living in a prison within my own mind and some things posted on social media is a trigger but I'd never say anything.

I've seen the memes and jokes about Bill Cosby and RKelly and it's a trigger but I won't say anything. I overhear conversations and I scroll past the posts because I didn't have the strength to admit … I'm broken. Please understand, I am not making this post for pity because truth is, I've had this jotted down in my notes for months yet I've just found the courage to share it. Yes, you've seen the video of me that has gone viral and you've heard the rumors but that isn't my truth.

Here's my truth … I'm broken.

Here's my truth … I'm gay.

Here's my truth … I've been sexually abused.

Many of you have seen the #metoo posts but tonight I'm adding to it with #mentoo because I was a victim of sexual molestation, from thirteen to nineteen. Now, I'm speaking out to stop the predators who prey on young men, especially in the church.

Am I ashamed? Not anymore.

Am I still broken? Yes, but I'm healing.

That is why, I can finally share my predator's names.

Pastor Jeffrey 'Jimmy' Griffin (my stepdad), Bishop David Wayne Page and Pastor Mark Anton, Sr. (his friends).

I am not sharing this for fame or monetary gain, I'm sharing this because I've finally gotten to a place of strength to even admit what happened to me. For those of you who are going to ask, "Why now," because damn it, it's time!

I'm sure this post will get a lot of attention, good and bad but it's my truth and I don't need your permission to share it. Those men are monsters and I know, for a fact, I'm not the only one broken by them.

This is my truth and tonight, I'm becoming free! Tonight, I begin to heal from my brokenness and I will no longer be a victim. I'm taking back my power and coming out of darkness.

2 Corinthians 3:17, "For the Lord is the Spirit, and wherever the Spirit of the Lord is, there is freedom."

#mentoo #victimnomore #brokennotdestroyed

Gwen

I am sitting in the middle of the bed with my iPad and tears are streaming down my face, as I read Jacque's status.

It's interrupted by a FaceTime call from him.

"Hey you."

"Hey," I reply, sniffing.

"You saw my status? I hope you're not disappointed or ashamed that I didn't tell you before I posted it. I mentioned your dad's name and—"

"Jacque, I'm so proud of you," I tell him, wiping my face. "And you didn't need my permission to declare your freedom. These are happy tears because you finally found your voice to be you."

"I never thought I'd say this but I don't know what took me so long. It feels like a weight has been lifted from my shoulders and for the first time, in a long time, I don't feel guilty."

I chuckle.

"What?" He asks.

"I can't believe we're finally having a civilized conversation. Two months ago, I wanted to strangle you and now—isn't it amazing how powerful prayer and therapy is?"

"Amen," he replies before we both laugh. "It's really good to hear you laugh Gwen. I know we've been through a lot, these last six months but I'm glad to know you're doing well."

"It was either wallow in self-pity or get up and survive. I got that from Dr. Sharpe," she smiles. "Seriously, I am getting better every day because I chose to survive and no matter what we've faced, I have to believe God has a purpose for all He's allowed us to go through. Plus, I realize things aren't solely about me anymore. I have this fellow to worry about." She moves the phone to show me her baby bump.

"I was reading my Bible, this morning and it says in Psalm thirty-four, verses seventeen through twenty, *'when the righteous cry for help, the Lord hears and delivers them out of all their troubles. The Lord is near to the brokenhearted and saves the crushed in spirit. Many are the afflictions of the righteous, but the Lord delivers him out of them all. He keeps all his bones; not one of them is broken.'"*

"Listen to you, quoting scripture. Hallelujah!"

We both laugh before he gets a serious look on his face.

"Jacque, what's wrong?"

"Gwen, I hope you can understand why I'm choosing to not be a part of the baby's life but I just don't want to mess him up."

"To be honest, I don't but this is your battle to fight and your demons to face because you are the only one who knows what you can handle. My prayer, is for the both of us to be healed. I don't know when or how that process will be but I'm trusting God to change your mind and your heart."

"I'm just not there yet, Gwen. I wish I was but I have too many unresolved demons that I need to deal with. One of them is Mark. He's been calling me nonstop and I don't want to bring that drama to you or our son's life. He doesn't deserve it and neither do you. Instead, I'll rather move out of the way and allow you to find someone who can be a better father to him than I can be."

"I'm not going to do that because you're his father and I believe, with the proper help and time, you'll be what he needs. I get it Jacque, you're afraid but how do you know what kind of father you'll be, if you don't try? You aren't David, Jimmy or Mark's father and you don't have to be the things they did to you. You're going to be a great dad to this little boy, who Dr. Lea says is almost five pounds with a lot of hair. You don't get to give up on him Jacque. As for Mark, you need to get a restraining order."

"I don't know if it'll do any good with me being here and him there. I'm praying he moves on."

"If he does, good but it can't hurt to talk to somebody about it in case he doesn't."

"I'll think about it. Anyway, I'll be flying into Memphis on Thursday and I plan to rent a small van to get the rest of my things from the house."

"What time is your flight getting in and do you need me to pick you up from the airport?"

"Yes, that would be great and if it's no bother, can I sleep in the guestroom."

"Um, now you're pushing it." I say.

"I'm sorry, I—"

"I'm just playing," I say laughing. "Yeah, it's cool."

"Thanks, I don't know what I would have done these last two months without you. And Gwen, I am truly sorry, for everything. I know I should have been honest with you, from the beginning but I didn't know how. I'd spent, all my life, living a lie and became great at pretending by patching up my broken pieces. It didn't matter how many times they'd inwardly cut me, as long as I could keep the bleeding hidden."

"Jacque, we were both broken and good at covering but I believe our brokenness was what drew us together and no matter how things are now, we had some great years together. Although, there are some things I regret, meeting you isn't one of them."

"Thank you for saying that and you have to know that I don't regret meeting and loving you either. You were, no you are the best thing that ever happened to me and I'll love you in this lifetime and the next."

"Dang mane, why are you trying to make me cry again? You know my hormones are all out of whack. But I love you too and thank you for being here these last twelve years. Though our paths are going in different directions, now, they'll always be connected."

"Because there is love worth fighting for," he says. "Goodnight Gwen, I'll see you in two days."

"Goodnight Jacque."

Jacque

Removing my headphones, I put everything back in my bag as the plane prepares to land. A while later, walking to baggage claim, I check my phone to see a text from Gwen. I get my bags and walk out, looking for her.

I see her waving.

Before I can get to her, I hear somebody call my name. I stop in my tracks.

"Mark? What are you doing here?" I ask looking over to Gwen. "Wait, how did you know I'd be here?"

"I'm not stalking you, if that's what you're thinking. I was walking in when I saw you coming out and I wanted to speak."

"You're catching a flight with no bags?"

"Jacque, wait. I'm sorry." He touches me but I jerk away from him. "Why are you being so cold and hateful towards me? I've apologized for everything and I even got the charges against you dropped. The least you can do is say thank you."

"Thank you? Thank you for what, ruining my life?"

"Are you still stuck on that? Man, I told you that was Haley, not me but you got a job now. A good job so shouldn't that count for something."

"How do you know about my job?"

He smiles, "did you think you got it on your own? Oh sweetie, Mark did that." He says, referring to himself in third person.

"Wow. I should have known. Well thank you but no thanks. I don't want or need your handouts because they always come with conditions. Look Mark, I'm trying my best not to be upset at you but things between us are over."

"You don't mean that," he says moving closer and I take a step back.

"I do because we're both screwed up and for so long, our brokenness has been the thing holding us together. Nevertheless, it's time we sever those ties and move on without any hard feelings."

"That's it?"

"That's all I have to offer."

"We can't even be friends?"

"Mark, don't make this harder than it has to be. Go on with your life and I'll do the same."

He looks up with tears in his eyes. "You're right Jacque. We've been dependent on one another because of what we went through, as boys. I wanted to give us another try but I see now it isn't what you want so I'll leave you alone. I've decided to take a position with the military, in Germany, far enough for me to forget you but close enough to be here if you ever need me."

"Mark, take care of yourself."

"You too Jacque."

I walk over to Gwen's car.

"Hey, how was your flight?" She asks, giving me a hug.

"It was good. I hope it wasn't too much trouble, getting through this traffic."

"No, I was already out because of a doctor's appointment."

"Everything good with you and the baby?"

"Yes, he is great and so am I but you're driving back because I'm tired," she smiles.

I walk over to the passenger side and open the door before getting in on my side. We drive, for a little while in silence until Gwen's phone vibrates. She opens her eyes to look at, whatever it is before she gasps.

"What's wrong?" I ask her.

"You all have matching tattoos?"

"What?"

She turns the phone around for me to see the picture. "You and Mark," she says with tears in her eyes. "You have matching tattoos?"

"Gwen, it's not what you think. Okay, yes, we have the same tattoo but—did he send you that?"

"What does it mean?"

"It's not—"

She holds her hand up to cut me off. "What does it mean?"

"Soul tie in Hebrew."

"All this time, you've been lying about that tattoo. Wow, this relationship or connection between you and Mark, is sicker than I thought."

I squeeze the steering wheel.

"You don't think I know that!" I take a deep breath then exhale. "Gwen, I'm sorry, I didn't mean to yell at you but I've tried to break away from Mark. I know it's not healthy but he will not leave me alone. Why do you think I took the job in Houston?"

"Running isn't going to fix it and we both know this because we've been running all of our lives. However, I do know that if you really wanted to sever the ties, you would."

"I don't know how. I've blocked him, ignored him and moved on but it will not go away. What else am I supposed to do?"

"Sever the ties from the head because a snake can survive with having his tail cut. If you want to truly be free from him, it has to start at the head."

"He said he's moving to Germany to work for the military and maybe this will be what we both need."

"A plane ride away isn't severing the ties," her voice trails off. "Maybe that's what you want, though. Look Jacque, if you don't want to end the relationship, you have with him, don't. This is your life and your decision but don't expect me to be okay with it, especially after our child is born because I won't."

"Gwen, I do want to end this because I'm tired. Mark and I have been a crutch for one another that it feels weird to walk without it, so you instinctively reach for it. Yet, it isn't good for us anymore and the only way we can learn to live without the crutch, it has to be destroyed."

"You keep saying us and we."

I look at her, confused.

"You keep referencing you and Mark when you are not responsible for him. Jacque, you have a responsibility to heal you."

"I feel guilty," I tell her, "because he was there for me when nobody else was. I don't know how to let him go."

She touches my arm. "I don't either."

I pull up to the house and park in the garage. When we get in the house, she turns back to me.

"I'm going to lay down but Pastor Magnolia is having a special prayer service tonight at the church.

It's not the magic answer, to your problems, but it can be a start. If you want, you are more than welcome to come with me."

Prayer Service

Gloria, Jacque and I walk into the sanctuary and there are over 100 people there.

"Hey, thank you all for coming." Pastor Magnolia says, greeting us as we walk in. "Jacque, it's so good to see you again. I hope you've been able to find a nice church home in Houston."

"Not yet but I'm looking." He says.

"Don't stay away from the assembly too long because it gives the enemy time to roam." She tells him.

"I won't."

We take a seat, near the front and after a few minutes, Pastor Magnolia stands in front, on the altar.

"Good evening High Point. I know it's not customary for us to have prayer on a Friday night but there's so much happening, in our city and land that God placed it on my heart to open the doors tonight. I don't know about you but I believe there is power in prayer and power in numbers.

Bible shares in Ecclesiastes four, verses nine through twelve," she says opening her Bible, '*Two people are better off than one, for they can help each other succeed. If one person falls, the other can reach out and help. But someone who falls alone, is in real trouble. Likewise, two people lying close together can keep each other warm. But how can one be warm alone? A person standing alone can be attacked and defeated, but two can stand back-to-back and conquer. Three are even better, for a triple-braided cord is not easily broken.*' Amen."

"Amen," the congregation says.

The praise team is there and they begin to sing.

"*We're all gathered here, in your presence Lord with our arms open wife. With lifted hands and open hearts, we welcome you to abide. Oh Lord, we need your spirit, your holy spirit right now. We can't do nothing until you come, dear Lord. For we are so unworthy to even call on your name.*

So please, Lord hear our prayer and don't let our coming be in vain."

"Anybody come yearning for the spirit of the Lord to fall fresh on you tonight?" The worship leader asks. "I know it's Friday but I've lived long enough to know that you might now make it to Sunday. So, will you worship with me tonight?"

She begins to sing again.

"Spirit, spirit, fall fresh on me. Spirit, spirit, fall fresh on me. Fall down, fall down; fall fresh on me."

The praise team repeats it over and over until they are barely whispering. While the music plays, Pastor Magnolia begins to pray.

"Let those of us who believe in the sovereign power of our God, touch and agree on one accord," Pastor says. "Our Father of heaven and earth. You, who are all-knowing, the giver and taker of life and the author and finisher of our faith.

You, God, created everything and this is why, we can stand boldly before your throne seeking you. God, I ask that you speak through thy servant with words of power, hope and faith. For God, it is today we need you to cover and protect because the enemy, in natural and spiritual form, is on attack.

God, he's attacking families and when he attacks one, he attacks all. Your word says that when we are in need, we can ask and you'll do. Your words say, when one is sick to call for the elders. Well God, we are here now and we're asking of you, these things. Give strength to the members and leaders of High Point who came to pray when called. Then master, protect your sheep from the prey.

Give provisions for those who are broken and can't find their way, heal the wounded and quiet the storms of those who are suicidal. Loosen shackles, God, heal hearts, suture up any open wounds, destroy curses, wipe slates clean, clean up bloodlines, remove hatred and deal with those who seek to hurt who belongs to you.

God, I need you to shield and protect, deliver and set free. Yes, we know things happen. Yes, we know we must endure, sometimes, but your word says if I pray and ask in faith that it shall be. I'm asking of you God to calm the winds and rescue your people. God, let there be no more devastation and pour out blessings that all which has been lost shall be restored.

God, you are able and I have no doubt that you can do it. Therefore, I'm standing, loudly proclaiming, for it is by your power that I can. Let the manifestation of your power be seen and Father," she pauses. "And Father, if any harm shall come our way, I pray that you don't allow it to stay.

God, we didn't come here tonight to play but we came to slay the giants of generational curses, the weapons of wounding words, the senseless killings on our streets, the innocent lives that are being taken and the slander being slung at your sheep. It's not ours to question but whatever your will is or has been, give us the power to overcome.

We thank you God for doing things we cannot see, for shifting things man cannot stop and for faith to stand even when it hurts. Give peace now because darkness cannot prevail. We know you can and we believe you will. Shine your light God, for darkness must cease. We thank you God and we're believing you to be mending broken pieces right now because we know you're able. Thank you, God. Thank you for Jesus and thank you for the obedience of your people. Amen."

Those around are speaking in tongue and others are still praying.

She walks over to Jacque.

"Jacque, God has not left you alone, no matter what the enemy wants you to believe. He told me to tell you, the enemy is on the attack but you can shut him down with your mouth. Speak your truth, even when it hurts because you've been silent too long. He says, the door of the prison is open and you can now come out."

She stops and the Holy Spirit intervenes causing her to speak in tongue before she continues. "That crutch, the one you think you can't walk or live without, God is giving you strength to balance without it but you'll have to let it go. This time, when you release it, God is going to also remove your guilt. He says, your debt is paid."

She then turns to me and places her hand on my stomach.

"Gwen, God has magnified your seed. The same seed you didn't think could grow, God watered. You had doubts about being a mother but God is removing your shame. All He needs you to do is trust Him. The baby you're carrying, God says his name shall be Jason Ezekiel. For Jason means one who cures and Ezekiel is the strength of God. With strong biblical names and the power of prayer, he shall be greater than anyone in your generation. Do you hear me?"

I'm crying so hard that all I can do is nod.

"Gloria, God isn't ashamed of you then why are you ashamed of you? You are His, He created you. In fact, before you were even a thought to your momma and daddy, God was thinking of you. Now is the time for you to get back to your rightful place. Come out of the mourning clothes because that period of your life is over. Your biological daddy may have left y'all but your spiritual father hasn't gone anywhere. Come out because it's time you lived for you."

She leaves us all, a weeping mess as she goes to a few other people.

I don't know how long we stay there but it was the right amount of time for heaven to hear our request. When we finally get ourselves together, to leave, I see Jacque is messing with his phone.

"You okay?"

"Yea, I'm trying to find that song they sang. Do you know it?"

"It's called Spirit by Luther Barnes."

Gwen

The next morning, I get up early to help Jacque pack the rest of his things before our meeting with Dr. Sharpe. When I walk in the living room, he's sitting on the couch with his laptop and a blank look on his face.

"Hey, what's wrong?"

He turns the computer around and I see David doing an interview. He removes his headphones and turns the volume up.

"Mr. Page, there have been some serious accusations against you by a man named Jacque London. Do you mind speaking on those?"

"All I'm going to say is, he's a liar. That young man is married to one of my daughters, neither of which I've had a relationship with in over twenty-five years."

"What happened between you and your daughters?"

"I don't want to talk about that but know, it was not because of me."

"You seem to be innocent in everything." The interviewer states.

"When you serve a God like I serve, He gives new mercies every morning. Whatever has happened in the past, is things I cannot change but I will not tolerate being lied on and used."

"Used? For money?"

"Money, fame or whatever he's seeking but it will not prosper. Ma'am, I've been an upstanding citizen, a man after God's own heart and a pillar of this community. Don't you find it strange that he will try to attack and defame my character, now?"

"Are you implying that someone is paying him to sabotage your election for President of the National Baptist Convention?"

"Of course. Church is as bad as politics. See, the enemy always comes out when you're at the cusp of your blessing and I can't be mad because that's what the enemy does. However, I won't be silenced. I have never molested anyone a day in my life and I'll go to my grave saying it."

"Thank you for your time Bishop—"

Jacque stops the interview.

"That man can lie when the truth is staring him in the face and he's good at it. He's sad and pitiful and has the nerve to call himself a bishop. I call bull-crap."

"Yea, well, I won't be silenced either." He says.

"What are you going to do?"

"Exactly what Pastor told me to. I'm going to use my mouth to tell my story."

"Are you sure, you're ready for that? You saw all the comments, email and messages from your last post."

"I'm tired of pretending like this man isn't a monster. He and his friends ruined our lives and as men, we always tend to keep stuff quiet. Not anymore. Bart is dead because of them and the sad reality, it could have easily been me or Mark because we've both spiraled out of control before. I must do this."

"Then I'll be here supporting you. In the meantime, we're done talking about that man because we need to get these boxes packed before our appointment with Dr. Sharpe. That's if you still want to go."

"Of course, I do."

When it came time to leave, I wasn't feeling good. I told Jacque I would cancel the appointment but he insisted on going without me. I watch him leave before I call Gloria.

"Hey," she answers. "Are you headed to your appointment with Dr. Sharpe?"

"No, I let Jacque go because I told him I wasn't feeling well."

"You okay?"

"Yeah but did you see the interview with David?"

"Girl, I saw that crap and God should have blown him up on camera."

"Did you notice who was standing behind him?"

"Behind him? No, who?"

"Your mother."

"I know you're lying!" She screams then I hear screeching tires and car horns.

"G, are you okay?"

"I had to pull over. Now, tell me again, who was standing behind him?"

"Go back and look at the video. I could be wrong but I am sure that was her. Do you think they've been messing around all this time?"

"I don't know but I'm going to find out. Get some rest and I'll call you back."

Gloria

I pull up in my mother's driveway, so fast, I almost hit the garage. She has the door open before I can get there.

"I take it you've seen the interview."

"Mother, please tell me you're not supporting this monster."

She doesn't say anything while stepping back to let me in.

"Mother?"

"Gloria, don't start with the dramatics."

"I'm dramatic because I want to know why my mother is standing behind a man, she divorced over twenty-five years ago. A man who left you for your best friend and a man, you know, is molesting boys. Mother, if that makes me dramatic then you're flat out dumb."

"Watch your mouth, in my house," She snaps. "I'm still your mother and you're going to respect me."

"When will you start respecting you?" I follow her into the living room. "Mom, what's really going on?"

"A few years after your father left, I almost lost this house. I never told you or your sister because it wasn't your problem. Anyway, David helped me to save it but it came at a cost."

"What cost?"

"I could never say anything about his past."

"So, your silence was worth a four bedroom house?" I question.

"What else was I supposed to do Gloria? I had two children, no job and I was barely able to keep up with everything the two of you needed."

"You were supposed to sell this damn house and keep your dignity! That man walked out on us and then treated us like we were scum of the earth. He broke us and never even bothered to come and check to see if we'd survived. Yet, now it all makes sense. He didn't need to come back because he'd already bought you. What I don't get is, why are you still supporting him? This house has been long paid for."

"He can still take it from me," she cries.

"Let him! Hell, you can move in with me or go to one of these retirement communities. Anything has to be better than being under his thumb."

"That's easy for you to say, when you've never had to suffer." She barks. "I did what I had to do to support you and your sister and I'm sorry if you can't appreciate that."

"You want to talk about suffering? Mother, we did suffer. We suffered every time we had to hear you crying over a man who could easily walk out on all of us. We suffered through years of not knowing how worthy we were because the only man we knew, broke our hearts and didn't care.

We suffered at the hands of men and women who lied liked they loved us and we couldn't tell the difference because nobody ever taught us what real love looked like." I stand up. "Mother, do you even know how broken your daughters are?"

"Gloria, I did the best I could, for you girls. You were never homeless, hungry or without. You had clothes and shoes—"

"We also went through hell!" I yell at her. "All those times I left home, going to Jennifer's house, it wasn't because I liked her that much. I went to her house because her mom was turning me out, in their basement."

"What?"

I wipe the tears that were now cascading down my face. "Yes mother, I'm gay and I was turned out by my best friend's mother who lived right across the street and you didn't have a clue."

I look out the window, across the street to that house.

"It started out, innocent, at first. She would be in the room when Jennifer and I were changing clothes and she'd touched me, not inappropriately but still touching. The night you and David told us about the divorce, I went over there, forgetting Jennifer was with her dad for the weekend. Her mom let me come in and as I cried to her, she consoled me.

Then she offered me a wine cooler and another until I was laughing and dancing around the room. When I fell back onto the couch, she kissed me. I tried to stop her but it felt good because somebody was finally paying me some attention. That night, she did things to me I'd never had done before and she would continue over the course of ten years."

I stop and turn back to my mother. Her mouth is open and she's crying.

"I didn't know," she says.

"You didn't want to know."

"That's not true. I love you and Gwen."

"But you love David more. Isn't that right? How else can one man have that much control over you, after everything he's done?"

"Because I know where his bones are buried," she yells. "I know his secrets and if I don't keep quiet, I can be in just as much trouble as he is."

"You knew he was molesting boys? How long?"

She cries harder.

"HOW FREAKING LONG MOTHER?"

"I found out when you were fourteen."

"That's two years before you all divorced and you didn't do anything to stop him. You allowed him to molest, God knows, how many boys and in the church you helped him to plant. Wow! You're just as sick as he is."

"No, I'm not."

"YES YOU ARE! You could have stopped him. You could have kept him from damaging boys who would grow into being broken men. Mother, their blood is as much on your hands as it is David's. Goodbye."

"Gloria, wait."

I turn back to look at her.

"Please tell Gwen and Jacque that I'm sorry."

"Tell them yourself."

Restoration Session

Dr. Sharpe

"Dr. Sharpe, I cannot thank you enough for meeting on a Saturday."

"When it comes to therapy, there are no set times. Is Gwen joining us?"

"No ma'am, she got sick before we left the house and I didn't want her to cancel, so I came on. I hope that's okay."

"I'm fine with it as long as you are."

He nods.

"Let us pray. Dear God, we thank you for allowing us to see another day. Now, as we gather in this place of restoration, we ask you to have your way because we know that with you, all things are possible.

Have your way, in this room, that we don't leave here the way we came but better, wiser, stronger and on the path to being restored. These things we pray, amen."

"Amen."

"Jacque, how was your move to Houston?"

"My move was good. I didn't realize how much it was needed until I got there."

"Why is that?"

"I guess because nobody knows me. Here, it feels like somebody is always watching and that keeps me tense."

"Tell me about your childhood."

"I was born in Detroit but moved to Memphis when I was, um, about five. My mother was a single mom who was so much fun. She loved to celebrate life, every day. She'd be the one to start a water fight, in the house or play silly pranks. Our house was painted with these bright colors and she made being a kid, fun. She always smiled, no matter what happened and people relied on her because she was the strong one. She was that mother that consoled all her friends or family members, when they were going through."

"You light up when you talk about her however, I feel there's a but coming. What happened to change your childhood?"

"My brother died when I was nine, from Leukemia. We moved to Memphis because his condition required treatment at St. Jude and after about a year, he was cancer free. We were all so happy because we'd spent so much time in and out of the hospital. One morning, mom went to wake him, for school, and he was gone. The doctors said his heart was tired and had given out. My mother was devastated and when he died, a part of her did too so she stopped celebrating life."

I don't say anything because I can tell he isn't done.

"A year later, she met Pastor Jeffrey Griffin."

"You emphasize the word pastor, why?" I ask him.

"Because he was great at throwing it around but he was a liar. At first, Jeffrey was cool. We went to church and he acted like he loved me and my mom. I was happy because she seemed to get the light back in her eyes but then, I turned eleven. It seemed like something switched in him overnight and I had to start calling him Jimmy."

I pause. "He'd noticed the small things that my mom didn't."

"Like what?"

"I didn't like for my clothes and shoes to be out of place, I didn't want to play sports, my room was always spotless and he said I carried myself in a feminine way. So, when I turned eleven, he'd make me go on these camping trips with two of his friends and their sons. He called it, making me a man. The trips were cool, at first but when I turned thirteen, the camping trips changed."

"What happened?"

"They molested us," he pauses. "In the middle of nowhere because they knew nobody would hear our screams."

"How long did it last?"

"I stopped going on the trips when I turned sixteen but the abuse didn't stop until I was nineteen. By that time, I found the strength to fight back because I'd had enough. When I turned twenty, I left and never looked back."

"What about your relationship with your mom?" I ask him.

"That ended the day she chose him over me."

"Is your mom still alive?"

"To be honest, I don't know and I've often thought about reaching out to her, for closure."

"Jacque, if you need closure, take it but you don't need permission from somebody standing on the outside of the door to shut it. Think about it," I tell him, getting up from my chair and walking to the door.

I open it.

"This is the door and on the outside, is where your past lies dormant and if the door is closed, it stays that way. However, as soon as you open it, things start moving. You start being kept up at night because things are moving. You can't concentrate because things are moving. You can't really hear well because you're bothered by the things outside the door. Guess what?" I shut the door. "I can close this door without any permission from who or what is on that side. You want to know why?"

I twist the lock.

"Because I control the door." I go back over and sit down. "Jacque, you control the door to your past and your story. Take it back and tell it, your way."

"Thank you, Dr. Sharpe. That illustration put a lot of things in context for me and from now on, I'm controlling my door and my narrative."

She smiles.

"Can I ask you one last question?"

"Sure."

"How do I get over guilt of wanting to let someone go who was there for me, during my darkest moments?"

"By getting over it. I know that seems harsh but the reality is, you aren't obligated to continue paying a debt for something that should have never had a price on it. A true friend, lover or spouse will never make you feel guilty over what they've done for you. Not when it comes from a genuine place."

"You're right."

"Jacque, you have the right to be free from whatever or whomever. Don't let guilt keep you hostage in a situation you have the power to come out off."

"Thank you, Dr. Sharpe."

"You're welcome and I hope the referral I gave you is working out."

"Yes, she's cool and she is helping me to face my fears."

"I'm glad to hear that but don't hold back. Therapy only works when you and the therapist work together. So, stay in therapy, put in the work and trust yourself."

"I will."

"Let me pray before you leave." We stand. "Dear God, we thank you once again for another chance to be restored. Now, Father, I ask you to watch over this young man who is taking back his power. God, protect him from the evil ones who seek to do him harm.

Shut their mouths and place stumbling blocks in their path. And God, if they happen to make it through, don't let whatever they try prosper. Allow Jacque to make it back to Houston safe for he is yours God, and by your might, he shall be what you've anointed him to be. We thank you and we seal this prayer by saying amen."

Jacque

Gwen was feeling better, by the time I got back, so we decide to go out for a late dinner since I'm leaving in the morning.

When we get in the car, I turn to her. "What do you have a taste for?"

"Really Jacque? How long have you known me and you still ask that question like it won't take all night to decide?"

"I'm buying, you decide."

She rolls her eyes. "Hmm, there's a new restaurant on Getwell Road, called Mary B's that I've been wanting to try."

"Was that hard?"

"Just hush and drive. Oh, how was the session with Dr. Sharpe?"

"It was really good but I have a feeling, you let me go by myself."

"I don't have a clue what you're talking about."

"I bet you don't."

***

"Welcome to Mary B's, is there just the two of you?"

"Yes," Gwen answers.

"Right this way."

"You have some nerve!"

Gwen and I both turn at the sound of an angry voice.

"How dare you walk around like you haven't ruined my life?"

We turn to see her father, David. She looks at me and we both turn to walk off.

He moves in front of us.

"You've ruined my life spewing lies all over the internet. How dare you think you can just get away with that?"

"Sir, you need to leave." The hostess says but he waves her off.

She quickly walks to the back of the restaurant.

"David, we both know I haven't lied on you. You and your friends are all child molesters and you've been getting away with it for years."

"YOU'RE A LIAR!" He yells. "And I will not allow you to destroy me."

"Nobody has to destroy you David because you're doing a fine job of it, yourself, by standing in the middle of a restaurant, yelling while reeking of alcohol."

"You shut up! Nobody was talking to you." He points in Gwen's direction. "You should have kept your faggot husband quiet!"

Some people in the restaurant gasps as others record.

"Wow. Is that what they teach you in the school of bishops, these days?" Gwen says. "I know you make God so proud."

By this time, management is running over. "Sir, we're going to have to ask you to leave before we call the police," he tells David.

He turns to him and yells, "I'm not going no got-damn where! I have a right to be wherever I want."

"You can but sir, you don't have the right to throw racial slurs around. Not in my establishment. I get you're upset but you've had too much to drink and unless you want to spend the night in the Desoto County jail, you need to call an Uber and leave."

"Gwen, let's go. Ma'am, we're ready." I tell the hostess, grabbing Gwen's hand.

"Don't you hear me talking to you, boy? Don't turn your back on me."

He snatches me by the back of my jacket and before I could catch us, we both stumble backwards and Gwen falls into a table. People scream and jump up to help and I turn around and punch him.

I continue to punch him until someone pulls me away. I rush over to Gwen and her eyes are closed.

"Gwen, baby, can you hear me? Please wake up."

"I think she hit her head, when she fell." A lady says. "I'm on the phone with 911."

***

Gloria comes running into the room.

"Where is she?"

"She's gone for a CAT scan."

"Oh my God Jacque, what happened?"

"Your father happened."

"What? Where did you see him?"

"Gwen wanted to try this new restaurant and he was there when we walked in. He was drunk and belligerent and when we tried to walk off, he snatched me by my jacket. She fell before I could catch her."

"This isn't your fault."

"Yes, it is. I keep hurting her. If I would have never put that post on Facebook, we wouldn't be here."

"No Jacque, you will not do that! You will not feel guilty about standing in your truth. This isn't on you. David did this."

"I know but if she loses the baby or dies, I'll never forgive myself."

"She won't."

A few hours later, we are leaving the hospital. The nurse was able to bandage my hand which had a few cuts from punching David. Gwen has a slight concussion but the baby wasn't hurt and we were all thankful for that.

I get her home, only after promising Gloria, I wouldn't let anything else happen to her. Gwen asked if she wanted to come to the house but she refused which was odd because Gloria never turned down helping her sister.

"Will you come into the bedroom while I take a shower?" Gwen asks. "The doctor said I needed to be watched for a few hours."

"Of course, as long as you're not uncomfortable."

She turns and looks at me. "Boy, we've been together twelve years so there's nothing on me that you haven't seen naked."

"Gwen, did you notice anything different about Gloria, tonight?"

"No, like what?"

"I don't know, she seemed off."

"I'll call her in the morning but I'm sure it's nothing."

When she gets out the shower, I'm standing at the door. She goes on to oil her skin, put on her underwear and I'm still standing there. She looks up and I have tears, in my eyes.

"You okay?"

"You were wrong?"

"What do you mean?" She inquires, confused.

"You said there's nothing, on you, I hadn't seen naked. You were wrong. I've never seen your stomach."

She puts on her robe and walks over to me. Grabbing my hands, she places them on her naked stomach.

"You feel that? That's your son. The son who will be strong and mighty and the one who will carry your legacy and your last name."

"But I'm gay."

"So what? Does that limit your abilities to love your son?"

I shake my head no.

"Does it stop you from loving him unconditionally, even if it's from afar?"

I shake my head no.

"Then this, Mr. London, is your son."

I burst into tears before falling to my knees, wrapping my hands around her and laying my head on her stomach.

Gwen

I roll over when I hear someone beating on the door. I look at my clock and see it's almost 8am. The door to the guestroom opens, so I get up and grab my robe. Walking down the hall, I hear Jacque's voice raise and then I see police officers getting ready to put him in handcuffs.

"Whoa, what's going on?"

"Ma'am, you need to step back. We have a warrant for this man's arrest."

"This man has a name and what's the warrant for?"

"Aggravated assault."

"Are you kidding me? When did you all start serving warrants on a Sunday because I know there is no judge issuing warrants for an aggravated assault on Saturday night?"

He doesn't say anything.

"Gwen, baby, don't get upset." Jacque says. "I'll handle this when I get down to the station. Can you call a lawyer?"

"I'm not upset but you aren't going anywhere until one of them produces the actual warrant for your arrest."

Neither of the officers say anything. I walk over and grab my phone.

"What are you doing?"

"Checking the warrant system. If you have one, it'll be there."

"Ma'am, that's not necessary," one of the officers say.

"Oh, now you speak. Well, speak into that radio and get a supervisor out here."

"Ma—"

"SU-PER-VIS-OR!" I sound out.

Twenty minutes later, another officer pulls up.

"Good morning, I'm Captain Cortez, what's going on?" She asks looking around.

"I don't know but maybe you can help me understand why your officers are here to arrest my husband. They say he has a warrant but we were the ones attacked last night. If anything, the man who attacked us should have been arrested."

"Where's the warrant?" She asks them.

Neither of them says anything.

"Ma'am, give me a minute."

She takes the two officers outside. I can't hear what she's saying but I see a whole lot of neck rolling and finger pointing. She comes back to the front door.

"There's obviously been a mistake. There is no warrant for your husband."

"I figured as much and I thank you for coming out but I'm going to need their name and badge numbers."

She takes a card from her pocket and writes some information down.

"Thank you."

I missed church and Jacque was late getting on the road because we were down at the police station filing a report on the officers and pressing charges on David. We both knew this was something David was controlling and we're refusing to allow him to control anything else.

We did find out that although David was detained on last night, at the restaurant, they didn't arrest him so I put that in the report as well.

"Thank you for having my back." Jacque says, when we walk into the house. "There's no telling what would have happened had I left with them."

"I know and the gall of David to think he can get away with paying police officers to do his bidding. Hell, they hadn't even been on shift a whole hour."

"How do you know so much about police work?"

"Um hello, I watch the First 48. I'm just pissed they didn't arrest him. I could have died or even lost the baby."

"I know." He sits down on the couch and lays his head back. "That's why I think it's time I did more than post on social media."

"What are you thinking?"

"Do you know anyone from the news or mainstream media? Anyone willing to do an interview to set the record straight," he inquires.

"Yea, I'm cool with Jasmine from Channel 4 News, let me call her. When are you thinking on doing it?"

"You're leaving for Gatlinburg, when?"

"December 29th."

"Can we do it that Friday before? That will give me time to fly back into the city."

"Let me call."

I call Jasmine and she jumped at the chance to interview Jacque.

"Friday, December 28th at six," I tell him.

"Thanks," he says getting up. "I'm going to put the last of my things in the van.

When he's done, I walk him outside and give him a hug.

"Have a safe trip. Text me updates so I'll know you're okay."

***

Jacque made it back to Houston and I was so relieved. I'd been praying the entire time because I didn't know what else David had up his sleeve. Especially now that the video, from the restaurant, is making its way across social media. It's been on KevOnStage, Ghetto Church News and it's only a matter of time before it reaches the National Baptist platform.

As for the charges we filed on David, he turned himself in but was released not even an hour later. I went to one court appearance and it was more of a show for him. The judge reset it until February but I knew, some kind of way, he'd get out it.

In the meantime, I'm not about to let him ruin the trip with my sister.

A few days later, Gloria is here to help me pack for our trip, this weekend but she's been a little quiet.

"G, are you alright?" I touch her arm. "Gloria?"

"Huh, what did you say?"

"What's up with you? You haven't been yourself since the night at the hospital."

She pushes my clothes over on the bed and sit down. I join her.

"Talk to me."

"I went to see mom, the day you told me about the video. I asked her why she would support a monster and it turns out, she knew David was a child molester."

"Wait, I think I'm having a pregnancy brain moment because I can't grasp what you're saying."

"First, she claimed, it was because he saved her from losing the house but then she admitted to being afraid of getting in trouble for knowing, all this time."

"How long has she known?"

"Since I was fourteen," Gloria answers.

"That's two years before they divorced."

Gloria

"Right," she says. "She thinks because she gave him a divorce, it fixes everything. Sister, I'm so angry I can spit fire. They don't even care about what they've done to us."

She comes over and pulls me into her.

"All these years I've hated David when I should have been hating her too." I have my fist balled so tight that my nails are breaking the skin. Gwen squeezes me harder when I try to push her away.

"No G! No," she fights. "You are always there for me, let me be here for you."

"Just let me go. I need to get out of here."

"I will not let you leave here like this. Let me help you."

"You can't! How can you help me when you're just as damaged?"

This time I push a little harder than I meant too and she squeals, in pain, releasing me.

"I'm sorry sister. I didn't mean to hurt you."

We both get off the bed.

"Gloria, tell me what's really going on," she begs. "What happened to you?"

I sit on the couch in her bedroom and she sits on the ottoman across from me.

"Do you remember all the time I used to spend at Jennifer's house?"

"How could I not? You were over there more than you were at home."

"The night we found out about the divorce, I went over there but Jennifer was gone with her dad. Anyway, Ms. Gambling let me in because I was crying and a whole ball of mess. When I was done, she gave me a wine cooler. She said it would help calm me. Then she gave me another and another. Man, I felt good."

"G, please don't tell me this woman raped you."

"Sister, you can't rape the willing."

"But you were sixteen," she states.

"Yea but I was also lonely and heartbroken."

"I don't understand. You always acted like nothing bothered you, even the divorce. You kept on with your life like you were fine."

"What else could I do? You were a mess and as my baby sister, I had to be what you needed and I allowed her to be what I needed. She took care of me, kept money in my pocket and treated me like she cared. I would later find out she didn't but by that time, I was too far gone. I was in love with that woman."

"When did it end?"

"When she sent me to jail for stalking?"

"What?" She squeals. "When was this?"

"I was twenty-one, I think. She'd moved on and gotten remarried but I was in love with her. And baby, if you thought you were bad, I was worse. I'd sneak into her house and leave my underwear under her pillows or be in the back seat of her car when she got off work. Oh, it was bad but going to jail snapped my ass out of that, quickly."

"How did I not know this? Wait, was that when you claimed you were backpacking with some friends?"

"Girl, I was backpacking alright. Downtown at 201 Poplar. I did thirty days in jail and I vowed to never go back."

"Is that why you're gay?" Gwen inquires.

"Maybe or maybe not; hell, I don't know."

"I'm so sorry I wasn't there for you. I never thought you needed me because you were always the strong sister."

"You're only as strong as your foundation and we both know, our foundation ain't worth nothing. That's why, when we get back from Gatlinburg, I'm going into an inpatient program."

"What kind of program?"

"For depression as well as intimacy and sexual struggles. It's a thirty day program in Arizona."

"Arizona? G, you couldn't find anything local?"

"I could have but knew I'd never take it serious, if I did it here. But don't worry, I'll be back before you have the baby."

Her eyes fill with tears.

"Don't cry sister."

"These are happy tears. I'm proud of you for taking the step to getting healthier and healed."

"I'm proud of us," she corrects, "for taking the steps to getting better. 2019 has to be greater than this."

Interview – Jacque

"Good evening and welcome to a special edition of Channel 4 News with Jasmine Loren. Today, my guest is Mr. Jacque London and his wife, Gwen. Mr. and Mrs. London, for the sake of transparency, you all called us for this interview. Is that correct?"

"It is," Gwen replies.

"Are we paying you for this interview?"

"No."

"Are you under any contractual agreement to conduct this interview?" She questions.

"No."

"Great, then let's get started. On behalf of Channel 4 News, we thank you for trusting us to tell your story," she says.

"Thank you for agreeing to sit down with us because we know there has been a lot of things said and shared on social media and it's time we spoke." I say.

"You're referencing the post, you shared, a few weeks back on social media? Is that correct Mr. London?"

"Please call me Jacque and yes, that's correct. I shared that status because I was, am, tired of being silent. I was a victim of sexual abuse."

"You named some of the largest and most known men in ministry. Were you not afraid of the backlash?"

"To be honest, I was more afraid of my behavior had I remained silent. Jasmine, you're right, I did name some men who have been named noble, by their communities but truth is, they aren't who they've made people believe." I tell her.

"Before we get into that, Mrs. London, is it true that Bishop Page is your father?"

She clears her throat. "Yes, he is but he said in an interview that it was not his choice as to why there is no relationship and he's a liar. My father left us when I was twelve, for my mother's best friend, who happened to be married to his best friend. His new wife prohibited him from having a relationship with us and he didn't. He walked away and never looked back. The first time I've been in his presence was a few weeks ago, when he showed up here."

"Is that when you found out about his relationship with your husband?"

"There was no relationship," Jacque corrects. "I met, Wayne as I called him, when I was eleven because he was friends with my stepdad and they took annual camping trips. He made me go as a way to make me a man. It was cool, at first, because his friends had sons my age."

"Did the abuse start on that trip?" She questions.

"No, it didn't start until I was thirteen. On that trip, when it was close to bedtime, Jimmy told us we were going to play a game. The game consisted of pulling a poker chip from this bowl that determined what tent we would sleep in that night. I don't think it clicked, really, what was happening until the tents were zipped." I pause. "From then on, things changed at home."

"What about your mother?"

"My mother knew but refused to do anything because it meant she'd have to give up the lifestyle he provided. So, I started acting out, rebelling and running away. When I turned twenty, I left and never spoke to my mother, Jimmy or Wayne, as I called him; again. My first time seeing Wayne or David again, was when he showed up at our house."

"Why are you speaking out now when it's been over twenty-five years?" Jasmine asks.

"Truthfully, I never had intentions of ever telling anybody about my past, not even my wife. I was ashamed of what happened to me and I vowed to take it to my grave. Then that video went viral and people degraded me for being secretly gay with a wife. They called me names and said I was a liar and a fraud. Those who believed me, looked at me with pity, something I've never wanted.

One day, I finally grasped what I was doing to myself and my wife. I was living a lie and it started to become overbearing and I knew if I didn't release what I'd bottled up, I was going to explode."

"Why should we believe you, Jacque? All of these men are notable, God-fearing men who are overseers of some of the largest churches in their communities. They each have connections to Memphis, pouring countless dollars back into the community and they've even taken a stand against sexual abuse, of any kind. Why should we take your word over theirs without evidence?"

"I'm not asking you or anybody listening to take my word, I'm simply stating facts to the questions you're asking. You have to decide whether you believe it or not. However, I don't need yours or anybody else permission to state my truth. This is my narrative and I'm choosing to tell it, in my words and on my terms.

Sure, these men may be known in the community, they may hold prayer breakfasts and raise money and they may be good at being overseers of their respective churches but ma'am, they are not God fearing. When you fear God, you vow to do his sheep no harm. As for evidence, I gave your producer a USB, before we got started. Can you ask him to play what's on it?"

She turns back to look at him and nods.

"Just for the record, I wasn't aware of any USB nor do I know what it contains." She presses the earpiece, "and what you're about to see may be graphic in nature."

The video starts to play. Its pictures of young men, in various uncompromising positions. The only face, being shown, is Jacque's and the men. Then it cuts to a video. When it's over, Jasmine and Gwen's faces are both in shock.

"That video was the last night Wayne and Jimmy violated me. My mom was gone to a church conference or something and I was home with Jimmy. I overheard him on the phone with Wayne and I knew what they were planning. I had this old video recorder that I set up, in my room. When I heard them coming, I pressed record. As you saw, they both took turns that night."

"Why record, that night?" Jasmine asks.

"I had plans to make copies and send to everybody in the church but I didn't because then people would know what I allowed them to do to me. Instead, it has traveled with me, all these years."

"Wow," she stumbles.

"Jasmine, I have no reason to lie on these men neither am I doing this for financial gain or fame. I'm speaking out for the other young men whose lives they've destroyed and for those who are contemplating suicide, gone through with suicide or living in a prison, daily. I'm doing this for my friend, Bart who killed himself a few years ago and for another friend, who I pray will seek help."

"Jacque, what do you say to others who are victims of sexual assault and afraid of dealing with it?"

"Two things. You control your own narrative and when you're ready, speak out. However, don't feel bad if you choose not too but don't stay a victim because it'll only break you. The second, seek help."

"Did you seek help?"

"Thanks to my wife, I am currently seeking help otherwise I wouldn't be here. I'm seeing a therapist who is helping me walk the path of healing."

"Gwen, may I ask if you knew of Jacque's past and his sexual orientation?"

"No, I only recently found out and I was disgusted, sick and humiliated."

"With him or what happened to him?"

"To be honest, all of it," she answers.

"How has that affected your relationship with Jacque now?"

She looks at me and smiles. "It's been hard, very hard but we're managing. If you're asking, if we will remain married, the answer is no. Jacque and I, now realize, we were two broken people looking for someone to fill in those empty places. Although we've managed to accomplish that, for over twelve years, we did so from broken places. Now, we're healing and want the best for each other."

"Will you be friends?" She inquires.

"We are friends," I reply taking Gwen's hand.

"Is it true that you're pregnant, Mrs. London and is Jacque the father?"

"Yes and yes."

"Congratulations."

"Thank you," we both say.

"It was a shock but we cannot question God's timing."

"What's next for you Jacque and you Gwen?"

Gwen looks at me and I begin to speak. "I'm going to continue in therapy and live life with no regrets. I'm finding my way to happiness and back to God because I allowed anger to keep me away from Him. As for what the future holds, I don't know but I will not hold myself back from finding out. Not anymore."

Jasmine smiles and then turns to Gwen.

"The same for me. I have a little one to think about now and I can't be for him, what he needs, if I stay in this broken place. For years, I blamed my emptiness on David and although he's partly to blame, I didn't miss anything not having him in my life. I'm moving on."

"Well, there you have it people of Memphis and the world. Jacque and Gwen, I thank you for being open and honest with me. I pray you both find the peace and happiness, that your baby is healthy and able to see two happy and healthy parents."

"Thank you."

"Until next time, this is Jasmine Loren with Channel 4 news."

"And cut!" The producer says.

Jacque

I am back in Houston and to keep from being depressed about being alone for the New Year, I decide to cook dinner. I have a ribeye steak marinating, along with some Brussel sprouts and mac & cheese. Oh, and a bottle of red wine.

My phone rings with a call from an unknown number. It's the fourth one today and just like the rest, I decline it. I get ready to turn the oil on to cook my steak when the phone rings again.

I snatch it from the sink but then I see it's a FaceTime from Gwen.

"Hey," I answer with a big smile.

"Happy New Year!" She yells.

"Happy New Year, Jacque!" Gloria sings coming into the camera. "I hope you're not stuck in your apartment, all by yourself."

"Happy New Year ladies. Yes, I am home by myself but I'm getting ready to cook a one man's dinner."

"Let me guess," Gwen says. "Red wine, ribeye, mac & cheese and asparagus."

"Nope, Brussel sprouts."

We both laugh.

"How are you enjoying the mountains," I ask her?

"Oh my God, it's so beautiful. I don't know why I've waited so long to come here."

"Gwen, we have to go," Gloria hollers, "or we're going to miss the opening act."

"Coming," she says before turning back to the phone. "I wanted to call and tell you Happy New Year and that I pray this New Year, for you, is greater than any you've ever had. I know these past six months have been," she sighs, "hard, devastating, mind blowing and hurtful but they've also been eye opening.

Jacque, our lives may have changed but I do love you. Happy New Year, Mr. London."

I clear my throat. "Happy New Year, Mrs. London and I pray the same blessing to you as well as an added blessing of love, happiness, a healthy baby and joy restored. May this year be the beginning of newness and healing for you? I love you Gwen."

I hang up the phone and silently pray that God is listening.

***

I jump up out of my sleep, thinking the banging I was hearing was a dream but it isn't. Throwing the cover back, I get up and rush down the hall, turning on the light. Snatching open the door, I see Mark standing there. He's disheveled and it looks like he hasn't slept in days.

"Mark? What in the hell are you doing here?"

"Looking to get his ass kicked!" My neighbor across the halls screams before slamming his door.

"Happy New Year Jacque." He says pushing pass me, into the apartment, holding up a bottle of alcohol. "Do you remember the time we bought in the New Year in Miami?"

"Mark, what are you doing?"

"I'm here to help you celebrate. Where are the glasses?"

"Mark! Stop! You shouldn't be here."

"Why not? Have you already moved on? Do you have somebody in your bed?"

When he moves to go down the hall, I grab his arm.

"You need to leave."

He looks at me for a few seconds then moves around me. When I turn around, he quickly turns back and throws the bottle at me. I slide, out of the way and it crashes into the wall.

"I'M NOT GOING ANYWHERE!" He slowly states, "And you don't want me too."

"Mark, I'm not in the mood to play whatever game this is. I have to be at work in a few hours."

"What about me? HUH? You just throw me away like I'm a piece of trash, after everything we've been through. What about me, Jacque?" He begins to cry.

I relent. "Look, you can stay here, tonight, on the couch. But that's only because I don't feel comfortable letting you behind the wheel, to kill an innocent person. I'll get you a pillow and a blanket but you have to leave, in the morning."

He slumps down on the couch.

I go to the hall closet to get what he needs.

"Thank you and I'm sorry for coming here like this."

"No problem, just get some sleep."

I go back into my bedroom and close the door, locking it.

My eyes pop open when I feel something heavy on me. I try to move but can't.

"What did you do?"

"Shh, I gave you a little something," Mark whispers, rubbing his hand over my lips. "Did you really think you could leave me? You can't leave me Jacque. You're my soul mate." He holds up his arm to show me his tattoo. "See, we're tied forever."

I close my eyes and he begin kissing me. On the lips then he kisses the tears, falling from the side of my eyes. He moves to my neck and then my chest. He moves down to my stomach.

"Mark, don't do this." I whisper.

"Shh, I got you."

I close my eyes and once he's done, he climbs back on top of me. "Man, I've missed you and I know you've missed me. Tell me you missed me."

I shake my head no.

"That's okay because I know you love me. I love you too."

He wipes the tears that are still falling from the corner of my eyes.

"I love you Jacque and I'll meet you over the clouds." He kisses me before raising up and slicing my throat.

My eyes pop open and I grab my neck, trying to remember where I am. It took a minute to comprehend it wasn't real. The same nightmare, I've been having for the past week. My phone vibrates, scaring me. I quickly grab it. It's another call from a private number. I press decline and look at the time.

4:02AM

The phone rings again. Same thing, no caller id.

I decline but it rings again.

"Hello," I answer agitated.

I hear crying.

"Look–"

"Jacque," a voice says. "Why are you doing this to me?"

"Mark, it's four in the morning? Have you been drinking?"

"Why won't you love me?" He slurs. "I need you."

"I cannot do this with you, right now. I'll call you tomorrow."

"Please Jacque—if you hang up, I'll kill myself."

I disconnect the call, trying to go back to sleep but I knew that was a long shot.

Gwen

Since the airing of that news special, with Jacque, life has been crazy. We've been bombarded with calls, to the office, from other news outlets, who wants us to appear but we've declined. Gloria said, "You better get that money," but it wasn't about that. Jacque's mission was to get the truth out and he did that.

Oh, speaking of getting the truth out, David has been removed from the church as he is being investigated. Thanks to Jacque's bravery, other young men have come forward, not only against David but the other two monsters too.

A lot of young men.

The sad reality, most of them were from their congregations. It broke my heart to know parents trusted their sons to the care of these men and they failed them. It's hard enough to get young people to worship and now, this has pushed them further away from God and the church.

I was getting my things together to leave the office for an appointment with Dr. Sharpe, when I hear a tap on the look and I look up to see Jacque.

"Jacque, what are you doing here? Are you okay?"

"I got in about an hour ago."

"Okay, that's not what I asked but what's going on? I haven't talked to you since I've been back and you look like you haven't slept in days, are you okay?" I ask walking around my desk. "Jacque, what's going on because you're starting to scare me."

"It's Mark. He tried to commit suicide."

I take a step back. "Oh."

"I know I should have called but I wanted to know if I could stay, in the guestroom for a few days."

"Let me get this straight. I can't get you to fly in for a doctor's appointment but you'll hop on the first plane, for Mark. A man you claim to be done with."

"Gwen, please." He yells. "I don't have time for this, right now!"

"Whoa, don't yell at me."

"Um, y'all are getting a little loud so I'm going to close the door," my assistant Tamar says.

"I'm sorry but I am tired of having this same conversation with you. I don't want to get attached to that baby."

"That baby?" I repeat. "Oh ok. Well, then yea, I'll help you."

"Thank you."

"I'm going to help your ass right up out my face. Get out of my office."

"What is your problem?" He questions with a shocked look on his face.

"You and all this drama. Jacque, you can do you and be with whomever you want but I will not keep holding your hand while you figure this crap out. If you want to be with Mark, be with him but I'm done. I've been giving you the benefit of the doubt, thinking you'll eventually come around, for the sake of our child but I see now, he isn't a priority."

"Is this really about the baby or you?" He snarls.

"Negro, are you serious? Do you honestly think I want you back, after everything? You're gay, boo and if you think for a millisecond, I'm that desperate for a penis, you're crazy. As a matter of fact, if were the only man within 2000 miles, I'd die dried up."

"Then why are you acting like a bitch?"

"Wow! I'm acting like a bitch because I show concern for the wellbeing of the man, I've been with for twelve years? If I recall, you were the one who said you wanted to "sever the ties," I say with air quotes, "not me."

"I do but he's obviously in a dark place, right now. Wouldn't you want someone to be there for you? Look Gwen, I don't expect you to understand but Mark is hurting right now and if I can keep him from dying, I will."

"Whatever Jacque. Do what you want but leave me out of it."

"I'm not putting you in it. I simply asked, out of courtesy, to sleep in the guestroom of our house. Hell, you're acting like I asked for a kidney. Mark was there for me in the lowest parts of my life and I'm going to do the same for him."

"Oh, we're back to the guilt syndrome. Fine, but I want no parts of it. I refuse to keep being drug into your mess with Mark and whoever else. We both know, you're going to come out of this, more messed up than you were. However, it's your life and your choice but from now on, please find somewhere else to stay."

"Gwen, I'm not trying to be disrespectful but that's my house too and if I want to stay, in any room I want, I damn well can. Now, I'll be staying in the guest room of OUR house for a few days. I will not bother you and I ask that you do the same."

"I don't even know who you are, right now. The way you're acting and talking to me but it's cool." I smile, grab my bags and brush pass him, out of the office.

"Gwen," he calls out.

"Tamar, I'll be out the rest of the afternoon. Let me know if our offer is accepted for the Turners."

"Yes ma'am."

I get in my car and press the start button, leaving the car in park while I search for a number on my phone. When it connects to the Bluetooth, I lay the phone on the seat and begin to drive.

"Holland Law, how may I help you?"

"Hey Mona, its Gwendolyn London, is Kameshia available?"

"Hey Mrs. London, she is. One moment."

I hold for a few minutes, while one of my good colleagues' answers. A few seconds of silence and Kameshia picks up. "Gwen, hey girl, are you ready to file them papers?" She laughs.

"As a matter of fact, I am."

"Alright then, I'll get started on them today and be in touch."

She hangs up and I continue to my appointment.

Restoration Session

Dr. Sharpe

"Dear God, thank you for another day of your grace and mercy. Father, we ask that you guide us today, like you've always done as we journey towards restoration. Use me, in your service that although Gwen sees me, she hears you. Allow her the strength to heal, as you see fit. We thank you God, amen."

"Amen."

"How are you?"

"Physically, Dr. Sharpe, I'm fine but the mental is where I'm having an issue."

"Why is that?"

"There are a lot of things," I sigh.

"Then let us unpack them. What's your biggest issue?"

"I had an argument with Jacque before I got here. He's in town because his friend, Mark, tried to kill himself."

"And you're upset about that?"

"Yes, because he said he was done with Mark, yet as soon as something happens to him; he's here in a few hours but he's never been to a doctor's appointment with me."

"Have you all talked about him being involved in the baby's life?"

"Yes, but he says he doesn't want to get attached out of fear of hurting him."

"And you don't believe him?"

"I don't know what I believe," she sighs.

"Then why are you so upset?"

"My son deserves a father! A father who will put him first before anybody else. A father who will love and protect him, be there when he's hurt, talk to him about relationships and this journey of life. A father who will be his role model and one who will not break his heart."

"A father, neither of you had." I say, interrupting her. "Gwen, what if Jacque isn't capable of being those things?"

"He has to be, doesn't he?"

"I think you know the answer to that."

She starts to cry.

"What are you so afraid of?" I question.

"That my son will end up broken, like me. Dr. Sharpe, many of my past mistakes were because my father didn't want me. I don't know why I couldn't pull myself up and go on about my life. I can't explain why I allowed myself to spiral out of control or why I searched for love in all the wrong places but I did. I wish I had the strength to allow God to mend what man broke but I didn't and I don't want that for my son. I've already failed him and he hasn't even been born."

"Gwen, not every child who is raised without a father turn out broken. There are plenty of men who go on to raise families because they vow to be what nobody was for them. Do you not realize the power, we possess? We have the power to speak and things happen. We have faith to move mountains. Gwen, your son doesn't have to repeat the sins of your past but you have to be willing to make sure he doesn't know them, to repeat them."

"How do I do that?"

"By fixing you and by stop blaming your father. Sure, your issues stemmed from him but you knew right from wrong. You, also, knew laying with those men weren't what you needed. At some point, you have to take responsibility for your brokenness because it's the only way you can heal. You can keep blaming your daddy but he's off living while you're here dying. Is that what you want?"

"No," she cries.

"Gwen, I know you want Jacque to be a father but that needs to be his decision, not yours. The last thing you should want, for your son, is a man who walks out on him because he wasn't ready to be what he needed. In the meantime, set boundaries. Don't allow Jacque to come and go as he pleases because the same way he doesn't want to get attached to your son, you shouldn't want your son to get attached to him. You have an opportunity to keep your son from falling victim to the same curses but it starts now. Stop looking behind you and move forward."

She grabs a tissue from the table next to her.

"I hear you and you're right. I'm going to set boundaries and demand a better life for my son."

"What's the second thing?"

"I'm worried about my sister. She's gone to Arizona to take part in a treatment program, for depression and sexual intimacy, when I didn't even know she was that sick. How could I not notice?"

"You were sick too."

"I know but she was there for me and a lot of the things she went through, I had no idea about."

"Did she want you to know?"

"No but I should have seen the signs."

"How? Would you know I had cancer by looking at me?"

"No."

"What if I told you I was molested as a child; do you see it?"

"No."

"What if I told you, I've had open heart surgery and there's a scar from the top of my chest to my naval, would you know that by looking at me?"

"No."

"We see what people want us to see and we know what they want to tell us. Gwen, you feel guilty about not being there for your sister but it wouldn't have done her any good. Just like Jacque, the both of you are broken so who would have healed who?"

"I get what you're saying Dr. Sharpe but knowing you have someone there, is help too."

"You're right but knowing and being are two, totally different things. Gwen, you've got to let yourself off the hook. You couldn't help your sister but she survived and is now getting help. You can't help Jacque but he survived and is getting help. Your biggest blessing, right now, is getting the help you need."

"You're right. I need to focus on me."

"What's your next thing?"

"My mother. We recently found out she knew our father was a child molester and did nothing about it."

"Gwen—"

"I know. I can't control a grown person. My mother has to atone for her sins, the same way I have too."

I smile. "You're listening."

"Yes, and I know what I have to do. I'm going to apologize to my sister for not being what she needed then, while being what she needs now. Then, I'm going to apologize to Jacque and set boundaries. As for my mother, I'm going to forgive her."

"Yes, progress. Great job Gwen and I am proud of you. Understand, change doesn't happen overnight. The longer it took to create the problem, the longer it takes to see a change."

"Thank you, Dr. Sharpe."

I stand. "Let's pray. Father, as we come tonight, we ask you to forgive us of our sins, those we've committed knowingly and unknowingly. We know that for us to receive forgiveness, we must forgive those who've hurt us. God, forgive. We know we aren't perfect yet we thank you for looking beyond our faults and seeing our need.

Now, as we prepare to leave this place of restoration, we ask that you be for us, what we need. Lead us, guide us, protect us and provide for us. Refill hope and dispel failure. Allow Gwen to forgive that she might walk in the purpose of you. Touch now and allow us to get home safely. We count it as well. Amen."

Jacque

I'm sitting next to Mark's bed when he opens his eyes.

His mouth forms into a smile.

"Hey," I say standing. "Would you like some water?"

He nods so I pour water into the cup and put the straw to his mouth.

"You scared me."

"I'm sorry," he whispers.

"Mark, what were you thinking? Why would you do this?"

He holds out his hand for me to take. I grab it and sit back in the chair.

"I needed you to come."

I release his hand. "You did this to get me here? Why?"

"You wouldn't talk to me."

"You didn't have to do this. What if you would have cut a main artery?"

"I knew what I was doing Jacque," he explains, pressing the button to raise the bed. "I didn't even cut myself deep enough. Besides, I've been here before, we both have."

"Which is more reason for you not to have done this."

"Then you should have talked to me," he shrugs.

"You need help."

"No, I need you and you came like I knew you would because you still love me."

"Where's Haley?"

"Who cares because you're here now and that's all that matters."

"Mark, stop. This is serious."

He rolls his eyes. "Jacque, quit being a wuss. My wound is superficial at best and the hospital will hold me, for a few days and then I'll be home. I was thinking of moving to Houston, since you seem to like it there but we'll have to find a house because I can't stay in an apartment. Ugh." He shudders. "You have some of the nosiest neighbors."

"How do you know where I live and about my neighbors."

"You don't remember?" He smiles. "I thought you were just acting like it never happened but you really don't remember."

"Remember what?"

"New Years. You'd cooked your favorite meal but you did Brussels sprouts instead of asparagus. I don't know why because they stink but it was your meal. Anyway, I got there before you did and I put a little something in that bottle of red wine you like. I don't know why you like that cheap stuff because it gives me a headache but I'll change that once we move in together."

"Mark!"

He smiles but then his face gets serious. "Do you know how long I had to hide in that closet before you finally drank enough to fall asleep? I was hoping you didn't hear the cracking of my bones but you didn't."

I'm looking at him with shock, anger, disgust and confusion.

"You looked so cute though, laid across the couch. I didn't want to move you but I did. I took you into the bedroom, undressed you and—"

"You tried to kill me."

He shakes his head. "You know I'd never kill you. I had to make sure you'd never leave me."

"No, no; you're lying. I would have remembered that."

"You were so out of it and for a second, I thought I'd given you too much of this stuff I stole from Haley's office. It's the stuff they give patients when they put them under anesthesia, you know, to keep them from moving. Whew! For a second, I thought you were a goner but then you woke up. I was so happy because it'd been so long since I've tasted you and ump, you still taste the same." He says rubbing his lips.

"You're lying, that was a nightmare. It wasn't real." I say getting up from the chair. "I dreamed you knocked on the door, I opened it and you were there. No, it was a dream."

"Yea, that part is because I definitely didn't knock and you surely didn't let me in. I did knock earlier which is how I know about your neighbors."

"You're lying!" I say again.

"If you say so but I'll be out of here in a week, tops and I'll have my real estate agent, not that little wife of yours, find us some properties in Houston to look at. You can go back since you have to work and I'll fly in once I'm released."

"You're sick Mark and need help. Let these people help you move on. Then go to Germany or wherever and get on with your life."

"There was no job in Germany," he laughs. "I can't believe you bought that lie. I was at the airport to see you."

"How'd you know I'd be there?"

"I always know where you are? Now, if you think we need help, maybe I'll go see that therapist you're seeing in Houston. Is she any good?"

"Stay away from me Mark. I mean it. Stay away."

"I can't do that. We're tied together, remember?"

"Please, I can't do this anymore. This is killing me. You have to let me go before I lose my mind. I'm begging you."

He sits up. "So you can go back to that bitch of a wife? Never! You belong to me and me only! We're soul mates and the sooner you stop fighting, the better it'll be for the both of us." He takes a deep breath. "Now, go because I need my beauty rest and I'll see you soon."

He lets the bed back down and covers himself with the blanket.

I get to the house and Gwen is in the living room, reading a book. She looks up when I come in but she doesn't even acknowledge me.

"Gwen," I call out to her but she bobs her head to whatever she's listening too so I take one of her headphones out.

"What are you doing?" She snaps.

"Can we talk?"

"Jacque, what's left to talk about? It's obvious your connection to Mark is stronger than you thought. That's cool, do you but you're right. I have been pressuring you to be a father because I thought it was what we both wanted, I won't anymore. As of this moment, I am done trying to fix you. My energy is going to bettering me, for the sake of my life and the life of my son and I'm sorry for trying to make you be something you're not."

"That's it? I don't get a say in anything?"

"Say, you'll sign the divorce papers when they're done."

"You filed for divorce?"

"Yes, no need in prolonging what needs to be done, right? This way, we both can get on with our lives. I'll put this house on the market and we can split the proceeds but I will not ask for anything financial, as it relates to me or this baby."

"This isn't fair Gwen. You can't just make all the decisions and say forget me, like I'm not a man. I am a man!"

She stands up. "Okay."

When she moves pass me, I grab her arm. "Don't walk away from me."

"Ouch, you're hurting me," she whines. "Jacque, let me go because you're hurting me."

I release her arm.

"I'm sorry."

She's rubbing her arm with tears in her eyes.

"I'm sorry Gwen, I didn't mean to grab you but you need to start listening."

"Who are you?" She asks. "Because I don't know this man standing in front of me. You look like the man I've shared my life with, these past twelve years but you definitely don't sound like him. What has happened to you?"

I don't reply.

"Jacque, you need some help."

"DON'T SAY THAT!" I scream at her with my hands balled into fists. "I'm not crazy."

This time she jumps. I look at her before going into the guestroom and slamming the door.

Gwen

It has been about two weeks since Jacque left. He was gone by the time I got up, the next morning after blowing up. He sent a text message, apologizing but I didn't reply. I'm done trying to figure him out, plus I realize, the only way I can fix me, I have to stop trying to fix him.

Gloria has been gone for almost two weeks, to her therapy program in Arizona. I talked to her, this morning, before I went to church and she sounded good. She has decided that Sundays will be the only day we talk because she doesn't want to become homesick. I will not lie; it has been hard not being able to talk to her, every day, but I'm happy she is finally getting the help she needs.

This morning, she asked about our mom and I had to admit, I hadn't spoken to her. A big mistake because Gloria made me promise to go by her house.

She's on this 'make amends' thing and I had to listen to her go on and on about it, until I agreed. I only had plans to call but since she wouldn't answer, I decide to drop by. Pulling up, across the street from her house, I get a call from Kameshia. I put my car in park and answer.

"Hey Kam, I hope you have some good news for me."

"Your papers have been filed but that's not why I'm calling. Have you heard from Jacque?"

"No, why?"

"I don't know if you're aware but one of my partners is the attorney for a father who is suing David for the abuse of his son. The grand jury indicted him, late Friday, on over thirteen counts of abuse, child pornography and child endangerment."

"Well hell, you should have started with this tea, honey, because it is way better than talking about my divorce. However, what does this have to do with Jacque?"

"He was supposed to call so that we can get a copy of the video of him and David but he hasn't responded to any of our calls or emails."

"Oh, okay but we haven't spoken since he was here, a few weeks ago but I'll reach out."

"That would be awesome. You can tell him I'll pay for him to ship it or I can send someone to Houston to make a copy of it. I don't care because that's just how bad we need it."

"Okay, I'll call him and let you know."

"Thanks Gwen. Take care."

When we hang up, I was about to call Jacque but the door to mom's house opens and David walks out. She comes out behind him, smiling like a teenager.

"You've got to be kidding me?"

When they embrace and kiss, my stomach turns. I turn off my car and walk to where they are.

"Well, isn't this lovely. Let me guess, you came by to give her communion?"

"Gwen, what are you doing here?" She asks, wiping her mouth.

"I was coming to check on you because you haven't been answering my calls but it looks like you're being taken care of."

"It's not what you think."

"Georgia, you don't have to explain anything to her. We're grown and can do whatever we damn well please." David barks.

"Yea, like rape innocent boys. Goodbye mother, hopefully you won't catch fleas from lying with this dog."

"Little girl, you don't need to be worried about me. Who you need to be concerned with is that gay husband of yours, the one I plan on suing for slander? You better hope I don't take that little business of yours, right along with it."

"Man, the only thing you can take is the virginity of boys who don't have the strength and power to stand up against you. I ain't them because I'm not scared of you. So, please do me the favor of coming after my little business and it'll be the last freaking thing you do. And you can't slander with the truth."

"Should I be scared?"

"Nope but you have been put on notice. You might have control over her," I say pointing to my mother, "and that gullible wife of yours but not me because I'll knock the hell out of you and then pray for your healing."

"You're right, I do have control because I got it like that. Maybe if you'd control your husband, he wouldn't want another man to bend him over." He laughs.

"What is it with my husband bishop? Are you still feigning for him? Are you still thinking about those camping trips and all the times he used to holler for help? No, maybe it's the satisfaction you get from breaking little boys. Is that it bishop? Do you find joy in destroying young men?"

"You don't know a damn thing about me but I know all about you Gwen. How you used to jump from relationship to relationship, being used by men for your body because you weren't worth shit else."

I smile. "Sir, if you think anything you say will get under my skin, think again. The fact remains, you're a monster. Jacque may be gay but he is who he is. You, on the other hand, are a filthy and pitiful excuse for a man. I hope you never get another restful night of sleep, knowing you had a hand in damaging him, every time you and your friends made him bend over.

You may be bishop to others but to me, you're nothing more than a child molesting, pervert who deserves to be under the jail. My prayer, you're the one who will be doing the bending, in the showers and cells of prison."

"That's where you're wrong, little girl, because I'll never do a day in jail. I have enough money and credibility to make sure of that. With all the connections I have in this city, nothing but my name will make it on paperwork in the DA's office. You can bet your house on that. I'm Bishop David Page and you can take that to the bank."

"We'll see, want we?"

Breaking News

Bishop David Page has been arrested following an indictment, by the grand jury, on charges of child molestation, child endangerment and child pornography. This indictment comes after video of him, molesting a young man, over twenty-five years ago, was released causing other young men to come forward. Prosecutors will not give details but a press conference is scheduled for tomorrow morning. Sources close to the Bishop's camp would not comment but we're being told, Bishop David Page will be arraigned on tomorrow.

"Did you see the breaking news story," Tamar asks coming into my office, the next morning.

"Yes, it's about time."

"Does it bother you that he's your father?" She questions.

"He hasn't been my father since I was thirteen years old so no, it doesn't bother me. I pray the judge throws the book at him because he deserves it. No man or woman has the right to violate a child but especially not a man who claims to speak on behalf of God."

"It's sad."

I nod. "Yes, but it's not my battle. My prayer now is for God's will to be done and justice given to all the victims."

Jacque

"Mr. London," Loreen says tapping on my door.

"What's up Loreen? I thought you were gone."

"Um, I was headed out but there's a man that keeps calling. He will not give me his name and when I try to take a message he hangs up and calls right back. I'm trying to switch the calls to the answering service, for the weekend but I don't want them to be bombarded with these calls. I'm trying not to get security involved but it's becoming a bit much." She says without taking a breath. "I'm sorry for babbling but I need to leave and I can't with these calls coming in, like this. What do you want me to do?"

"Do you know what number he's calling from?"

"No, it's blocked out. Sir, if he keeps on, I'll have to let Mr. Brady know." She says, referring to my boss.

"No, don't do that. I'll take care of it. You can go ahead and switch the calls to the answering service."

She leaves and I pick up my desk phone and dial Mark's number.

"Jacque, what a surprise," he sings.

"Cut the bullshit Mark. Why are you constantly calling my job? Are you trying to get me fired?"

"Hold on sweet face, I am not calling your job. What are you talking about?"

"My secretary said some man keeps calling, back to back and I know it's you."

"Jacque, I may do a lot of things to get your attention but this isn't one. Besides, I'm the one that got you this job. Do you need me to call Brady?"

"No, please don't do that. I need my job."

"Don't worry, he won't fire you but you need to let them investigate the calls because I can't have anything happening to you."

"I'm not your problem and I'm fully capable of handling my own business. For the last time, leave me alone."

"I love you too."

I slam the phone down. Turning back to my computer, I open my email and send a message to the security team to have them investigate the calls. Pressing send, I get a notification of a new email without a subject and the sender is listed as my name. I double click to open it.

"SNITCHES GET STITCHES!"

I hit reply, "MOLESTERS DESERVE BULLETS!"

Once I hit send, I forward the message to the spam address for the company. I shut my laptop and grab my jacket. Getting to my truck, my cell phone rings with a call from a blocked number. I throw it, along with my jacket into the back seat. I loosen my tie and head in the direction of downtown.

Pulling into the parking lot, of the first bar I see, I turn off the truck and go inside.

"What can I get you?" The bartender asks.

"Something strong."

"Long day?" The guy next to me asks.

"Long life, is more like it."

"Well, sit down and let me buy you a drink. I'm T."

I nod.

***

"Wake up Mr. London, it's time for you to go."

I open my eyes and wait for them to focus.

"What?"

"Let's go! Unless you want to spend another night with us."

I swing my legs over the side of the bunk and stand up.

"Where am I?"

"The Four Seasons. Where the hell does it look like? You're in jail, where you've been for the last 18 hours. Now move!"

The sound of the door, slamming, makes me cringe. The guy grabs my arm and leads me to a desk. Looking down, I notice I'm wearing my pants and shoes but a different shirt.

"Here are your belongings, sign here."

I do as I'm told before taking the brown envelope.

"What happens now?"

"Now, you go home and get your life together," the officer states. "You ought to be glad the judge decided to let you sleep it off instead of a fine, jail time or record. Get yourself together Mr. London. Next!"

I walk out the jail with no idea where my car is. I get my phone out of the envelope and wait for it to come on.

"Crap!" I mutter when I realize its dead. I walk over to the gas station and ask to use the phone. I look up a number for a cab company, make the call and hand the phone back to the guy.

"Excuse me, what day is it?" I question.

"It's Monday, February 4th at 5:30AM. Is there anything else you need?"

"Monday? Dang it!" I say. "Sir, can I please use your phone one more time?"

"Yea but make it quick."

I dial Loreen's number but forgot it rolls over to the answering service until 8AM. I hang up, praying Mr. Brady isn't in the office today.

An hour later, I make it home and after a shower, I set the alarm on the nightstand for 7:30AM before I plug up my phone and lay across the bed.

My eyes open and I try to remember where I am. I hear the constant vibrating of my phone and then … I leap from the bed to see it's after two. I press the alarm button on the clock and realize I set it for PM, instead of AM.

"No, no!" I slide down on the floor, beside the bed and grab my phone. There are notifications for voicemails, emails and texts. I open the text and see four messages from Loreen with the last one being an hour ago.

"Where are you?"

"Jacque, I'm starting to worry. Call me."

"Mr. Brady is on a war path. Answer your phone."

"Damn it Jacque. I'm trying to save your job."

I quickly type a reply to her.

Me: I'm so sorry but I'm just getting your messages.

Loreen: WTH?

Me: It's a long story.

Loreen: I hope it was worth your job. Check your email.

I open my email and the color drains from my face.

Subject: Notice of Immediate Termination

Dear Mr. London,

Our company, Brady Enterprises, is a company built on its reputation and integrity, not only of our executive board but employees too. Due to this, each employee agrees to honor this policy, on and off the premises. Considering current information, we've received, concerning your personal behavior, we are hereby releasing you from your employment with our company.

Usually this matter would have been discussed face to face, however you failed to call or show up today. Due to this, this letter will serve as your official notice of termination, effective immediately, from Brady Enterprises. A copy of this letter and all evidence of your unprofessional behavior, will be sent to you, by FedEx courier.

You can expect a separate letter detailing any benefits you are entitled too as well as a packet to mail back your badge, office keys and any other property of

Brady Enterprises. You will also need to keep us updated on your mailing address so that we can provide your W2 information in the future.

Regards, Larry Stall.

Director of Human Resources.

My head falls back on the bed.

Loreen: Did you get the email?

Me: Yea but what unprofessional behavior is he talking about?

Loreen: Dude, you were arrested for public intoxication. If that wasn't enough, your mug shot and a video of you arguing and fighting with some dude was sent to Mr. Brady. It's all being sent to you. I'm sorry Jacque.

Me: This is all on me. Thank you for letting me know.

I go back out of the thread with Loreen and see a message in the Unknown Senders box.

+1 (281) 713-5125: Thanks for last night. Whenever you're in need, call me. – T

I click on the attachment and it's a picture of me with the guy from the bar, sitting in my lap and licking my chest.

"Oh my God!" I mumble. "What in the hell did I do?"

I squeeze my eyes shut, trying to remember anything about that night but all I can see is T's face at the bar. I reply to the text.

Me: Hey, I know this is going to sound weird but can you tell me where we met because I have no memory of what happened.

I lay the phone on my chest and a few minutes pass before it dings with a response.

+1 (281) 713-5125: I'm not surprised, you were pretty wasted but we met at a bar called The Pastry War. Do you, at least, remember what we did?

Me: I'm sorry but I don't remember anything.

+1 (281) 713-5125: Then maybe we need to do it again because I sure do remember you. That's if, you didn't get into any trouble with your boyfriend. LOL!

Me: Boyfriend?

+1 (281) 713-5125: Yeah, the white dude you were arguing with when I left. You all were heated and going at it, in the parking lot. He was pissed, especially when he caught us in your truck. Don't worry, we were done but you didn't have on a shirt.

Me: I don't remember any of it but I guess that explains why I woke up in jail.

+1 (281) 713-5125: Jail? Wow, are you okay?

Me: Yeah, I wasn't charged with anything but apparently, I was drunk enough to spend 18 hours in a cell and not know.

+1 (281) 713-5125: Well, that's good because things could have been worse. Anyway, I'm headed into a meeting but you have my number now so use it whenever you want to let loose again. My name is Tristan, by the way.

"Mark was there?" I say out loud before getting up to get dressed. Sitting on the side of the bed, tying my shoes, I hear keys outside the door. By the time I make it from my bedroom, I see Mark walking in.

"Mark, what the hell?"

"Well, hello sunshine," he says closing the door. "I got you some coffee and pastries. I knew you'd need it after the weekend you've had. Here are your keys." He drops them on the table.

"No, that's not what I mean. What are you doing here?"

"Starting our life together. I was planning on coming later but after you called yesterday, I knew you needed me. Besides, it seems like I can't leave you by yourself or else you'll end up sleeping with random people in bar parking lots. Oh, I got your truck and I had it detailed. Ugh," he shutters. "You're just a mess but that's okay, I forgive you." He walks over and kisses me on the cheek. "But the next time you cheat on me, I'll kill you. I'm going to shower."

He leaves the room and me standing there, trying to rationalize what the hell just happened.

"I must be dreaming," I say turning around. "Yea, I'm tripping."

I start to walk to the bedroom, when my phone rings with a call from Gwen.

"Yea," I answer angrily.

"Um, is this a bad time?"

"No, what's up?"

"Are you okay?" She inquires.

"Gwen, what can I do for you?"

"Hold on, you don't have to bite my head off. I was only calling to check—"

"I don't need you checking up on me!" I snap. "I'm a grown ass man and capable of taking care of myself. Get off my back and stop calling me!"

I hear her gasp. "Wow. Had you let me finished, you would have heard me say, I was calling to check and see if you'd been contacted by the District Attorney's office. They've been trying to serve you with subpoenas but forget you! Bastard!" She disconnects the call.

"AHH!" I yell before throwing the phone.

Mark comes running out of the bedroom, naked.

"What happened?"

He touches my arm and I turn, pushing him away from me. "Don't!"

I grab my keys and wallet from the table, leaving out of the apartment to the sound of Mark screaming my name.

Gwen

I'm pacing the floor, livid at the way Jacque talked to me. I was only calling to tell him about the subpoena, the courts are trying to serve him as part of David's arrest but the fool blew up at me. I wish I could call Gloria because I'm mad enough to get on a plane bound for Houston, to knock the hell out of him.

"Mrs. London, are you ready?"

"Yes, I'm on my way."

I take a second to calm down before following Tajuana, of Gee Realty inside the conference room. I am speaking to a room full of women who are interested in a real estate career and I can't afford to allow my emotions to throw me off my game.

Once it's over, I'm sitting in a room, changing my shoes. Wearing heels are my thing but being almost 36 weeks pregnant, they are no longer comfortable.

"Excuse me, aren't you Gwendolyn London?"

I slide my loafers on and stand.

"I am and you are?"

"My name is Savita Ching with the District Attorney's Office. Do you have a moment?"

"Sure, but what is this about?"

"Your father, David Page."

I motion for her to sit. "What can I do for you Ms. Ching?"

"As you know, we're investigating your father—"

"He's not my father," I correct her. "He had a part in creating me but he's no father. Can you please refer to him as David?"

"My apology. The DA is currently prosecuting Mr. Page on a long list of charges and my job, as an investigator is to gather the evidence."

"Okay but what do you need from me? I don't know anything about David or his life. Until recently, I hadn't seen him in years nor was I aware of what he'd done to those boys."

"What about your husband? How has all of this affected him? What I'm asking, is he mentally stable to be a witness for the prosecutor?"

"Shouldn't you be asking Jacque about this?"

"Could you give me his contact information, like his phone number and address?"

I give her the side eye. "Give me your card and I'll pass your information on to him."

"That won't be necessary. Thank you, Mrs. London." She stands to grab her things. "Oh, has your father, I mean Mr. Page, ever violated you?"

"No, hell no. Why would you ask that?"

"I'm just covering all the bases because we don't want any surprises if this goes to trial."

"What do you mean if?"

"You have a great day."

On the way to the car, I call Kameshia.

"Hey, do you know of a Savita Ching with the DA's office?"

"Savita Ching? No, I've never heard of her but I can check. What happened?"

"She showed up at an event I had earlier, asking questions about Jacque and David. She wanted to know about his mental capacity and if David had ever violated me."

"That sounds like someone on David's side. Next time, ask for credentials and if you don't feel comfortable answering questions, refer them to me."

"Thanks, I wanted to ask because it was weird."

"Baby, they are doing all they can to make sure David doesn't do any jail time but the DA is great at her job."

"Did Jacque ever call?"

"No, have you talked to him?"

I tried to call him earlier and be blew up at me. I don't know what's going on with him but I'm out of it."

"Dang, I really need that video."

"Let me look through some of his things, he left here, to see if maybe there's a copy at the house."

"Thanks Gwen."

When I release the call, I get a pain in my stomach. I stop for a moment but when I walk, the pain hits again.

Leaving Dr. Lea's office, she tells me that what I'm feeling is Braxton Hicks contractions. They are common during this time of my pregnancy. However, she is concerned about my blood pressure. She wants to keep an eye on it, which means I'll have to stop in, every other day to get it checked. If it doesn't go down, she's going to admit me to the hospital.

I decide to pick up some food, from Newk's and head home. After eating and showering, I'm propped up in the bed reading the book, The Family that Lies: Merci Restored, when my eyes get heavy. I lay my Kindle on the nightstand and turn off my book light.

My eyes fly open when I feel the baby kicking. I groan and roll over to see that it's almost midnight.

"Calm down, little one."

A heaviness comes over me and I can't shake it, so I get up and begin to walk in circles while praying out loud.

"God, in my studying, I know that midnight is the hour of spiritual activity, it's the darkest hour and the hour when demonic activity is at an all-time high. God, I don't know why you've woken me up but I'm speaking against anything that is not of you. Whatever is happening, God you stop it. Whatever demonic force that is trying to overtake my family, cut it off at the head.

God, you said power of life and death is on my tongue. Well, I'm speaking death to the attacks, to the lies and to the hurt against my family. Tonight, in this hour, I am not afraid to cry loud, if it means saving my son, my sister, my mother, my husband, friends and anybody attached to me. God, tonight, in this hour, I will not be quiet when there is lives on the line.

You've placed Jacque on my heart and now I'm asking you to keep his mind, stay the hand of suicide and protect him from evil. God, I'm standing on faith, praying for you to loosen shackles and free him. You, God, have given me dominion and authority over all things so now, I'm putting on my armor to go to war. Not just for Jacque's life but for my life and our son. God, I'm decreeing that we shall not drink from the cup of suffering, no more this season.

We've endured enough and we need peace. Please God, release peace. And God, while I have your ear, watch over my sister and may she find the healing she deserves, all the way in Arizona. May she come back, happy, healing and on the path of being made whole. Bless Kameshia with open eyes and ears to be able to see what may have been hidden from her. Let her effectively do what is in her responsibility, while keeping her safe from harm. God, I trust you and I take you at your word. Amen."

Jacque

"What can I do for you?"

"I need a room?" I tell the scruffy looking Asian man.

"How many hours? You can get one hour for $35, two hours for $50 or the entire night for $75."

"Give me the entire night. Do you need my id?"

"Not unless you want it in your name?"

I put it back in my wallet, taking out the cash. "I'd prefer something on the second floor."

"Here, you'll be in room 24, on the back side."

I grab the key and head out to my truck. Pulling around back, I grab my bag and get out.

"What's up sweet stuff, you need some company tonight?" The girl asks. "I got something that can make you feel good."

"I doubt it but no thanks, I'm good."

"I'll be out here for most of the night, if you change your mind."

I go inside the room and lock the door. Turning on the light, the room reeks of stale cigarettes and old sex. I shut the curtains and put my bag on the table.

Sitting on the side of the bed, I kick off my shoes and grab the bottle of whiskey and pills from my bag. I pour a few pills in my mouth before taking a couple of long swigs from the bottle and laying back.

"AH," I jump up when water is thrown in my face. I open my eyes but the room is pitch black.

"Why are you ignoring me?" A voice demands to know.

"Mark?"

"Nope, try again," he laughs.

"Who are you and what do you want?"

"You don't recognize the voice?" He laughs. "It's me, your conscience, sweet Jacque."

"You're lying." I say, feeling around for the light. "Where's the light?"

"What are you trying to see? Yes, you're still in this dirty, run down motel with a gun, bottle of whiskey and pills. Isn't that why I'm here, to talk you out of doing something stupid?"

"Why are you doing this?"

"Me? You're bothering me with all this whining and crying. Weren't you the one who called for me Jacque? Well, I'm here now. Tell me what you want."

"I don't know."

"LIAR!" The voice booms. "Aren't you tired of lying? Truth is, you want me to tell you it's okay to splatter your brain on the walls. You want me to steady your hand and then hold you until you take your last breath. Don't you?"

"Do you think I need your damn permission? I don't need you or anybody else because I'm very capable of handling this myself."

The light pops on and I jump.

"Where are you?" I scream. "Where are you?"

"I'm where I've always been, in your head, but you can silence me by pulling the trigger. Come on Jacque, do it. Gwen will be better off without you anyway and we both know your baby boy will. Look at you, you're a plum mess. You can't say no to Mark, you're still afraid of David and you got so drunk last night that you had sex with a random stranger.

You're having the same nightmare over and over and it's only a matter of time before Mark kills you anyway. Well, if not him, it'll be David. Either way, you're dead so no harm, no foul, right?"

"Shut up!" I scream.

"You're broken and bitter, you're by yourself and scared and you've turned your back on your wife.

What else is there to live for? Pull the trigger and put us both out of our misery."

"SHUT UP! SHUT UP!"

"Make me Jacque. Make me shut up," the voice taunts. "Boo-who, for poor Jacque."

I grab the gun, remove the safety and put it to my head.

"That's it," the voice says clapping. "Finally, you're being a man."

"God, I'm so sorry. Please forgive me of my sins and for what I'm about to do. Please take care of Gwen and my son and if you're willing, receive me into your kingdom. I'm sorry for not being the man you created. Amen."

"Woo, that was sweet. Amen Jesus," The voice mocks.

I close my eyes and put my finger on the trigger.

"I'll count you down. 3, 2—"

"I can't!" I cry putting the safety back on and laying the gun on the table.

"Man, I knew you couldn't do it. Get your ass up, go back to Memphis and get the help you need."

"I don't have anywhere to go."

"Yes, you do and we both know where that is. Cut your losses, let your tail hang between your legs and go Jacque. If not, you'll be back here, dead by this time tomorrow."

"I don't want to die," I cry.

"Then get the help you need to survive."

I quickly throw my stuff in the bag and run out to my truck.

"Dude, you okay?" The girl asks looking at me funny when I get to the bottom of the steps.

"Yea, why?"

"You were in there hollering and screaming at somebody but I ain't seen nobody go in that room but you."

"Yea, I'm fine."

"Nawl, no you're not but you could be."

"What did you say?"

"You don't belong here sir. Go home," she says before walking off.

Gwen

I was up, earlier than usual, getting ready to stop by Dr. Lea's office because I'm having some spotting but no pain. I didn't want to call her because she told me, yesterday that if my pressure isn't normal, I'm going straight to the hospital but I had too. I'm praying everything is good because Gloria is coming home tomorrow and I promised her a home cooked meal.

Once I'm done showering, dressing and all the other stuff that's now taking me longer to accomplish, I'm headed out. I set the alarm and go out to get in the car. When I press the button for the garage to lift, I am shocked to see Jacque's truck.

I get out of my car and walk over to the driver's window. I tap but he doesn't move so I knock harder and he jumps up.

"Jacque, what are you doing?"

He opens the door.

"Gwen, I'm so sorry." He says pulling me into him but I push him off.

"How long have you been out here?"

"For about an hour. I drove, all night, from Houston and I didn't want to wake you."

"Look, if this is about you staying in the guest room, I am not about to argue with you because I don't need the drama. I'm trying to keep my blood pressure down so I don't spend the rest of this pregnancy in the hospital." I turn to walk off after telling all my business.

"Gwen wait, please." He says grabbing my arm. "I've really made a mess of my life and I need help."

"Good for you."

"No, what I mean is, I need your help."

She moves my hand from her arm. "Jacque—"

"I was going to kill myself last night," he says with tears forming in his eyes. "I had the gun to my head and I almost pulled the trigger but I couldn't. Gwen, I'm broken."

He falls to his knees in front of me and God allows me to remember, waking up last night and praying.

"This last month has been the worse of my life and I didn't think I was going to survive. Last night was the lowest I've ever been and without help, I might not make it."

"Jacque, get up." I help him stand. "The only way you can get the help you need; you have to get the help you need. I know that sounds crazy but I don't know any other way to say it. You can't do this for me, we aren't together and neither can you do it for this baby. You must want it for Jacque." I look at my watch. "I have a doctor's appointment and if I don't leave now, I'm going to be late. Why don't you take a shower and try to rest until I get back? I think you have some clothes still here."

"Can I come with you?"

"Don't do that."

"Do what?" He asks.

"Show up now that you've hit rock bottom. Jacque, I'm glad you've decided to get the help you need and I'll be here for you, but things are still the same with us. Right now, you're running off adrenaline. Sober up and if you feel the same about wanting to be a part of this baby's life then we can set boundaries."

I leave him standing there and continue to my appointment.

***

"Your blood pressure is good," Dr. Lea says.

"Thank you Jesus."

"You still need to take it easy. You're close to 37 weeks and your cervix has already dilated one centimeter, which is why you're spotting a little. What you experienced, this morning, was your body expelling the mucus plug."

"That's the thing that blocks the opening of the cervix?"

"Yes."

"Are you saying I can go into labor at any time?"

"No, I'm saying you're in early labor but it could be another two weeks before your cervix dilates any further. This is why I said, take it easy."

"When will the contractions start?"

"There's no definitive time but trust me, you'll know. Take it easy," she reiterates.

"Yes ma'am. Thank you, Dr. Lea."

"You're welcome and I'll see you next week, unless you go into labor before then."

I swing by the office to drop off some paperwork I needed Tamar to file and some blueprints for the contractors to pick up. When I walk in, the office is dark and I know she should be here by now.

"Hello," I call out when the lights pop on and everybody jumps out. "Oh my God."

"Surprise," they yell.

When they spread, I see Gloria.

"SISTER!" I squeal running to her. "I thought you weren't coming home until tomorrow."

"I lied, duh! You know we had to throw you a baby shower before this big head little boy makes his arrival."

"Well, it's a good thing you're doing it now because I've already started to dilate."

"Figures. He's like his mammy, impatient."

I push her and she burst into laughter.

"G, I am so happy to see you."

"Yea, I guess you are seeing you haven't kept me filled in on all the crap that's been happening."

"I didn't want to worry you."

"No, no you two. Right now, is all about the baby. Come," Tamar says grabbing my hand.

I spend the next hour and half opening gifts before they load them into mine and Gloria's car. She follows me home and when we get out, she's pointing to Jacque's truck.

"Um, I thought ole boy was in Houston with his pink girlfriend."

"He was until this morning but I don't know the details."

"Oh, I'll find out."

"No, G." I say grabbing her arm. "When he got here this morning, he was in bad shape. Not like he'd been beat up or anything but in worse shape than he was before. Let him be, okay?"

"Fine," she pouts.

We walk in and Jacque is in the kitchen, without a shirt on.

"Hey," he says swallowing some coffee. "I didn't hear y'all come in. I'll be right back."

"Damn," Gloria blurts. "All that fine body and a man gets to enjoy it."

"G!" I say, laughing and shaking my head.

"Don't act like you weren't thinking it too."

Jacque

I walk into the living room where Gwen and Gloria are sitting on the couch, laughing about something.

"Hey," Gwen says, "can you get those gifts out of my and Gloria's car? You can put them in the other room, right across from mine."

I walk out to the car and stop when I see all the baby stuff.

"You okay?" Gloria asks, coming up to me.

"Yea, but can I ask you something?"

"Sure," she says walking to the other side of the car.

"The program you went to, in Arizona, did it help you?"

"More than I can explain. The first night, I won't lie, I didn't think I was going to make it. Then I called

Pastor Magnolia, she prayed, I cried and I knew I had to stay."

"Why?"

We both stop at the front of the car. "Because, I was doing more damage to myself than anyone else could. I was allowing anger to eat away the good parts of me. I was so angry that I intentionally sabotaged anybody who showed an interest in me. I was in a mode of, leave them before they leave you but then I reconnected with Nikki and she wasn't going," she laughs. "Every time I bucked at her or tried to run her off, she stayed and I realized, I needed her in my life. However, that couldn't happen without this program. It saved my life."

"But you had to go to Arizona."

"I didn't have too but I chose too because it wouldn't have been easy to walk out of the program, being so far away. Plus, it was worth it. They offer all kinds of programs, small groups and individual sessions designed around your needs. They listen and what I loved, they didn't force me to do anything. Everything I shared or experienced, was my choice."

"I need to do something to get out of this dark space I'm in."

"I had to come and—I'm sorry, are you two actually having a civilized conversation?" Gwen says, interrupting.

"Whatever big momma, come and grab a bag."

Gwen rolls her eyes before snatching the bag from Gloria.

"Jacque, do what's best for you. If you want to give this program a try, I'll give you the number to the counselor who helped me. The great part, they answer calls 24/7."

"I'd like that."

We finished getting all the packages out of the car. Gloria leaves to head home because Nikki was waiting on her. While I put all the baby's things in the room, Gwen is converting to the nursery, she fixes dinner.

"Are you hungry?" She asks when I walk into the kitchen.

"Yes, and can we talk while we eat?"

"Sure."

She prepares our plates and I get us something to drink. I sit down and she holds out her hand to say grace.

"I got arrested," I blurt as soon as she says amen.

She swallows her forkful of pasta before looking at me. "Recently?"

I nod, yes.

"For what?"

"Public intoxication."

"Seriously Jacque? You hardly ever drink. What were you thinking?"

"I wasn't. Everything started to feel like it was closing in on me. I've been having nightmares about the molestation. Someone was constantly calling my job and I've been getting these crazy emails that I know are coming from David. On top of that, I can't get rid of Mark. He's everywhere and knows everything I do. Oh, I lost my job too. It's just too much."

"Jacque, why are you still fighting yourself? What do you want?"

I lay my fork down. "Gwen, I'm tired. I mean the kind of tired that would make me sit in a raggedy motel room with bugs and a smell signifying it hadn't been cleaned in years, ready to die. I didn't care about anything else, all I wanted was the hell, in my life, to be over."

"You keep saying the same thing yet you haven't answered the questions. Why are you still fighting yourself and what do you want? Before you answer, think about what Jacque wants, without putting anybody else in the equation."

"I want to be free," my voice cracking, "I want to be me and I want to be happy."

She gets up from the table and leaves out. A few minutes later, she comes back with a book and a notebook.

"Pastor Magnolia gave me this journal, a while back and I could never start to write in it and I know, now, you need it more than me." She pushes her plate out the way. "It's called Be a Fighter. Jacque, it's time you fight for everything you want. To do that, you first have to be free so, I'm going to give you the conditions of your pardon."

"My what?"

"When you've been in prison for a while, after being found guilty, the governor has the ability to grant you a pardon. Now, the pardon doesn't remove the offense from your record but you can no longer be held to the restrictions of your previous charge. In other words, a pardon forgives you for the crime you committed, either because you were wrongly convicted or the punishment you've received was too harsh for the crime."

"You got all of this from watching the First 48?"

She laughs. "No, I've been studying because I was in the place you are, not long ago and the only thing that gave me hope was this baby. At first, I couldn't understand why God would allow me to become pregnant, after all this time. I mean, my marriage is over, my husband was molested by my father, my sister is depressed and broken, and all hell is breaking loose. Shoot, this was the absolute worst time to be pregnant because I was broken and not fit to be a mother to a plant, let alone a baby but now, I know it was to save me."

I touch her hand.

"Too bad you can't get pregnant," she says causing us both to laugh.

Gwen

"God says and I wrote this down," I tell him, picking up the notebook. "In Romans eight starting at verse one, it says, *so now there is no condemnation for those who belong to Christ Jesus. And because you belong to him, the power of the life-giving Spirit has freed you from the power of sin that leads to death.*

The Law of Moses was unable to save us because of the weakness of our sinful nature. So God did what the law could not do. He sent his own Son in a body like the bodies we sinners have. And in that body God declared an end to sin's control over us by giving his Son as a sacrifice for our sins."

He lays his head on the table and I lay my hand on top of it.

"Jacque, I don't have all the answers but I know you need to be free because the time you've spent, paying for a crime you didn't commit, was harsher than you deserved. You've sentenced yourself to a lifetime of recycling the same dead stuff instead of destroying it. You've been carrying prison clothes, from relationship to relationship and place to place. You've been dragging brokenness yoked around your neck but it's time Jacque. Time for you to go free because you've spent too much time making yourself pay for the actions of others. You've overstayed your time in darkness, ashamed of what you've done."

I begin to rub his head. "It's time Jacque but only if you're ready."

"I'm ready," he sobs. "Oh God, free me."

I give him the time he needs to cry out his pain while I get my phone. I open iTunes and press play on a gospel song, I heard recently titled Deliver Me.

"*Lord, deliver me cause all I seem to do is hurt me, hurt me. Lord, deliver me cause all I seem to do is hurt me, hurt me.*"

I watch Jacque as he continues to cry. When the song gets to the part, he really needs to hear, I turn it up a little louder.

"Starting here, starting now, the things that hurt you in the past won't control your future. Starting now, this is a new day. This is your exodus, you are officially released."

When the song ends, I stop the music and walk over to him. "Jacque, these are the conditions of your pardon. Number one, you shall no longer walk in the counsel of guilt or shame. Number two, you must make amends to yourself. Number three, ask the forgiveness of those you've hurt. Number four, ensure you aren't pressured into accepting this pardon for anyone but yourself. Finally, number five, the number of God's grace; believe in you again because you've been graced to overcome. Do you accept the terms of this pardon?"

His cries get louder but I take both hands to lift his head.

"Do you accept the terms of your pardon?"

"Yes."

"Then it's final. This is your exodus or departure and you shall be free but you're only as free as you believe."

He stands up and pulls me into a hug.

"Whew!" He says releasing me. "I didn't realize how much I needed that but I'm grateful to you listening to God, even if it means me crying like a baby. How did you get so wise?"

"I'm not wise Jacque, I'm wounded and in being wounded, I understand now that God had to let me go down, to get up. See, God gave me this message, for me, while I was at the bottom of my pit. Yet, I couldn't comprehend it then, because I wasn't ready. Oh, but when I got tired, fed up and at the end of my rope; God reminded me of what He promised. Never to leave me nor forsake me. And this message, this thang preached to the depths of my soul. You're going to be alright," I tell him while picking up our plates to warm the food. "I need to tell you, it isn't over because the process is just beginning and it's going to hurt like you wouldn't believe. I know because I'm still walking the path but it's worth it."

When I come back to the table, he has this look on his face.

"What?"

"Would you hate me if I said, I'm still not ready to be a father?"

"As much as it hurts, no. Jacque, I'd rather you be honest, now, then to hurt our son later."

"You sure because you were so—"

"I was so blinded by what I desired. Jacque, I can't make you be what you're not but thank you for your honesty and your willingness to move out of the way for someone else to step in. Not yet but one day," I add, "because I'm not ready for another relationship right now."

"Thank you."

I smile at him.

"Gloria gave me the number for that place in Arizona and I'm going to call them, tonight."

"What about Houston?"

"I don't know yet. I'll see what happens after this treatment program."

"And what about Mark?"

"He isn't good for me Gwen and although I've always known it, my guilt wouldn't let me walk away."

"We both know he's not going to let you go that easy. Are you afraid of what he might do?"

"Not anymore. I'm tired of fighting and all I can do now, is trust God and the process."

"Amen."

***

It's been a little over two weeks and Jacque is still here, handling some things. He spoke with a lawyer about the divorce and because he isn't contesting it, it shouldn't be long to have it resolved. He also met with the District Attorney and Kameshia's team, the one suing David. Since his abuse was so long ago, he won't have to testify but the video is going to help.

David pleaded guilty to a lesser charge, for that night at the restaurant and will be placed on probation. I didn't feel like fighting it, I simply wanted him out of our lives.

Jacque, spoke to some of the young men, who were also violated and abused by David and his friends. He made a promise to come back, whenever they need him. I'm proud of him because I can see the glow returning to his face.

He said he might leave, today but wasn't sure. I've been laying here, for over thirty minutes, trying to go back to sleep. I have an afternoon appointment with

Dr. Lea but the baby has been kicking up a storm, all night and I've started to have a few contractions. I sit on the side of the bed, for a minute before I go into the bathroom.

Once I'm done, I knock on the guest bedroom's door to see if Jacque's up. When he doesn't say anything, I push open the door to see the bed made and a letter in the middle of it.

I walk over and get it, sitting in the chair next to the window.

Dear Gwen,

Please forgive me for leaving like this but I couldn't bear telling you goodbye. I know our relationship is at a weird place but you still allowed me in. Even after everything I've put you through and the way I talked to you, you still let me in and I can never repay you for that. You're dealing with the wounds of your heart and the brokenness, you've had to endure yet you stopped long enough to bandage me. Thank you.

I spoke with the treatment center in Arizona, they'll have a space for me in a week and I took it. I'm headed to Houston to work out something with my landlord about holding my apartment and handling the basic necessities; like electric and such, while I'm gone. I also have to deal with the issue of Mark. I'm surprised he hasn't been calling me, nonstop, since I've been here. I don't know it that's a blessing or a curse but either way, I'm taking the conditions of my pardon.

I love you Gwendolyn Page London and I pray you'll be able to find love again. Take care of yourself and our son. With your strength and God's love, he'll be born a conqueror. I'll be in touch, as we work through the divorce and if you need to sell the house, to create new memories, do it.

Oh, I got a call from the District Attorney, yesterday and if you haven't heard, David and Mark, Sr. are pleading *guilty to lesser charges that will include jail time. A small victory. One more thing, in my last session with Dr. Sharpe, she asked about my mom. I looked her up and she died three years ago. The obituary didn't list Jimmy so who knows if he is or not. For my sake, I pray he isn't so he can spend the last of his years in jail too.*

Anyway, I'll be in touch soon.

Until I see you again,

Love Jacque.

"Oh, Jacque." I say, wiping the tears. "Ah," I moan rubbing my stomach. Okay little dude, I'm not ready yet. Stay put."

I take the letter and put in on my nightstand before deciding to lay back down. Gloria has forbidden me from coming into the office and without anything else to do, I guess my only option is to sleep until it's time to see Dr. Lea.

Gloria

I woke up this morning, smiling. A big, huge smile because I feel great. After Gwen and I took our first trip to Gatlinburg, which was amazing, we've made a promise to make it an annual thing, every New Year. Even though, next year she'll have a baby and hopefully, I'll have a girlfriend seeing that Nikki and I have been spending a lot of time together; I am excited about our new tradition.

Since being back from treatment, work has been steadily increasing. Tamar told me, it's been this was since that news interview with Jacque and Gwen. I don't know what it is about airing your dirty laundry that makes people trust you more but I wasn't complaining about being swamped with work.

Gwen planned on working until the day she went into labor but being that she's already dilating and having Braxton Hicks, I refused to allow her to come in. Instead, we're going to utilize the services of some young ladies who are working toward their real estate license. This way, they can get some OJT or On Job Training.

I pull up at Gwen's house and grab the food I picked up. Using my key, I open the door and put the bag and keys on the counter before calling her name.

She doesn't answer.

"Gwen," I call again. Walking closer to her bedroom, I hear her screaming my name. I rush down the hall, into her bedroom and then the bathroom.

"G, my water broke," she cries.

"Why didn't you call me?" I ask, sitting the food on the sink and going to her.

"I couldn't get to the phone," she says before screaming.

I open her legs and see the baby's hair.

"Oh my God," I dry heave. "Gwen, when did your water break?"

"About an hour or so ago."

"And you didn't think to call me or 911? I can see the baby's freaking hair and you're acting like labor just started. Girl, hell! I ain't ready for this."

"Stop yelling," she cries. "It hurts."

"Hell yeah, it hurts. You got a whole human pushing through your stuff with no medicine."

I pull my phone from my pocket, dial 911 and put it on speaker while grabbing some towels.

"911, do you need Fire, Police or Ambulance?"

"All of them because my sister is in labor and I can see the top of the baby's head."

"What's the address, ma'am?"

"7452 Lions Gate Place, Memphis."

Gwen screams.

"Ma'am, please hurry." I tell her.

"What's your name?"

"Gloria."

"Gloria, if you're seeing hair then you're more than likely going to have to deliver this baby."

"Ma'am, the only deliverer I know is Jesus and he ain't here right now so can you hurry the professionals who know what they're doing?"

Gwen screams again.

"Gloria, I need you to stay calm and listen to my instructions. First, make sure the door is open for the EMTs."

"Okay," I say laying the phone down and sprinting for the front door. I get back, out of breath, "it's done."

"Good. What's your sister's name?"

"I can think of a few to call her but her government name is Gwen."

"Okay. How far along is Gwen?"

"She's 38 weeks."

"You're doing great Gloria. Next, I need you to place some towels under Gwen to catch any fluid or blood that will occur."

"Say what now?" I dry heave again. "Blood and fluid?"

"G, just do it." Gwen hisses.

"That's easy for you to say, heifer." I roll my eyes before getting the towels and spreading them under her. "Lift up. Ma'am, do I need to have her lay down?"

"Yes, it'll be easier."

"You heard her," I say motioning for Gwen to lay down. "Okay, Ms. 911 lady, it's done." I say, wiping my forehead with my sleeve.

"Now, wash your hands because you're going to have to feel around the baby's head once it's out to ensure the cord is not wrapped around its neck."

I dry heave, "do what?"

"Take a breath Gloria," she commands. "You can do this."

"Girl," I say slapping Gwen's leg before getting up to wash my hands, "you better be glad I love you. Got me all up in your twat. I like girls but you're my sister and this is just gross on too many levels."

"G, focus …. OOO MY GOOOOOODDD!" Gwen yells and I yell too. "G," she huffs.

"Yea, what?"

"Shut the hell up! You don't have a whole human tearing your coochie apart. Oh my God. I need to push."

"Make sure she's lying down." The operator says.

"She is," I respond, my breathing getting heavier as I'm trying not to throw up.

"Okay, have her grab her knees, pull them toward her chest and push hard."

"You," dry heaving, "heard her." I say patting Gwen's knee.

She grabs her legs and this time, she screams really loud until his head pops out.

"His head is out. Oh my God," I dry heave, "this is disgusting."

"You're doing good Gloria. Now, gently rub around his neck to make sure the cord isn't wrapped."

Dry heave.

"It's not," I tell her when I'm done.

"Okay, gently push his head toward her back and have her push, one more time."

I grab his head and tap her leg with my elbow then I dry heave. "You heard her."

"AHHHHHH!!" Gwen screams until the baby is in my hands.

"He's here. Gwen, he's here."

His cry fills the bathroom.

"Good job. Lay the baby on Gwen's chest or stomach and cover him with another towel."

I do that just as the EMTs rush in and I quickly relinquish my duties to them before sitting on the floor.

Gwen

The baby and I are transported to the hospital since I wasn't scheduled to have a home birth and because he was delivered, a couple of weeks before his due date. Dr. Lea is keeping us overnight, just to make we're good but the baby is amazing, all six pounds and six ounces of him is healthy.

I'm holding my phone, contemplating whether I should text Jacque.

"What are you naming him?" Gloria asks while rocking the baby in her arms.

"Jason Ezekiel London." I reply, deciding against that text, right now.

"Jason Ezekiel, I can see that but where did you get it? You been watching them white baby shows?"

I laugh and shake my head. "Do you not remember what Pastor Magnolia said that night, at the prayer service?"

"Baby, I was so slayed in the spirit, it took me forever to remember how to get home. What did she say?"

"She told me his name was going to be Jason Ezekiel. Jason means one who cures and Ezekiel is the strength of God."

"Oh wow, now that's cool."

"Yeah and it's also perfect because he's going to carry the power to cure our bloodline. Mine and Jacque's."

"Amen to that," she coos to him. "Happy Birthday, Jason Ezekiel. February 28, 2019."

✳✳✳

Four weeks later, Gloria and I are at my house preparing for the dedication of Jason. We decided to have it here, in order for it to be intimate and among family and friends. And I wasn't ready to take him out, yet. I invited Pastor Magnolia and a few members of High Point, along with Nikki to come help us celebrate.

"Have you talked to mom?" Gloria asks.

"Nope. I tried to call her but she didn't answer. I even sent her an evite for the dedication but she still didn't respond."

"I've tried to reach out too and she's been silent. Hell, I don't know why she's mad at us. She can have David and all of his demons, if she wants but I want no parts."

"Right and she can be mad all she want but I am not about to waste another minute trying to force something that doesn't deserve my time. My now is sacred."

"Okay then Evangelist Gwen. My now is sacred." She mocks.

"I'm serious G. I've spent too much time allowing people to get away with doing things to me and while I'm left broken and depressed, they've gone on with their lives. Baby, I am no longer allowing folk to eat with me, if their table manners don't match mine. I ain't churching with just anybody because our perspective of God may be different and I'm declining the invitations that aren't for me.

I'm protective of my NOW because I realize everybody who smiles at me may not be good for me. I'm defensive of my NOW because I don't need no dark spirits penetrating my home. And I'm unapologetic about my NOW because I'm sick of folk trying to tell me what I should have done when they weren't there the times I suffered alone."

"Dang Gwen, I was just kidding about the evangelist thing but are you sure you haven't been called to preach?"

"No way. This anointing came from a lot of late nights, wallowing in darkness and days spent in therapy."

"Speaking of therapy, are you done with it?"

"Heck no. I've spoken to Dr. Sharpe and I'll start back seeing her, in a few weeks."

She walks over and gives me a hug, just as the doorbell rings.

"Get the door before you have me crying."

Once everybody is here, Jacque walks into the living room holding the baby. He surprised us, this morning and although he isn't going to take the role of father, I'm allowing him to be a part of this.

Pastor Magnolia opens a book and begins to read, "We know the Lord gave you this child and now, we stand before His throne and an open heaven, dedicating him back to Christ. We also stand, in humble submission, vowing to teach him the Word of

God and what it means to live in faith. This is a way to share with other believers, our commitment to parenting this child in a godly manner and it's an invitation to keep us accountable."

When she's done, I raise the piece of paper and begin to read. "We want our child to be faithful to Christ, the church, and his family. Our desire, for Jason Ezekiel, is to live by faith and for God to make him brave, kindhearted, and gentle. We commit to raising him in a way that glorifies Jesus while giving him room to be who God has created."

I take the baby from Jacque who speaks next. "Our prayer, for Jason Ezekiel, is that he may be a spring of refreshment and life to all who cross his path and that he will love by the same love God has given him. We pray he will never have to question his value and never be embarrassed to walk in his purpose. We, further pray that we shall see all the blessings he will birth and that God gives the wisdom needed to raise him. More than anything, we pray that he will fall so in love with Jesus that he'll never give up, never lose hope, never be broken, and never be responsible for breaking others yet always loving, helping and whole."

Gloria goes next, "Our prayer for Jason Ezekiel is peace. Peace from the generational curses of our past. Peace from what has been connected to our bloodline and peace to never know what it feels like to be broken and rejected. You will survive and be strong and you will be who God has ordained. Jason Ezekiel, your auntie will love, spoil and raise you to the best of her ability until her dying day."

"Amen," we all say.

"Let us pray," Pastor says. "Our Father, we stand today, in the presence of your anointing, first thanking you. Thank you for restoration, healing and deliverance. Thank you for your peace and understanding that is always greater than ours. God, we've held the dedication for Jason Ezekiel but now we need you to cover him and all those who stand as witnesses.

God, we know how hard this journey can be. God, we understand how the pressures of this world can cause us to fall. God, we've seen how brokenness can claim your children but we declare that it shall no longer be so. For we declare him to be washed in your blood, covered by your love and surrounded by your hands. You've created this baby and you gave him, as a blessing, to the parents he deserves.

Give us, as the village, the provisions to teach him according to your word. For the Bible tells us in Mark nine and forty-two, *'whoever causes one of these little ones, who believe in you, to sin; it would be better for him to tie a millstone around his neck and be thrown into the sea.'* God, we vow to do right by this child. We thank you for entrusting him to us and we count it as well. If you believe, say amen."

"Amen."

Jacque

I stand at the baby's crib and watch him sleep.

"You okay?" Gwen whispers from the nursery door.

I wipe the tears from my eyes and walk towards her.

"I never thought I'd be here," I tell her.

"Neither did I."

She turns and I follow her into the living room.

"Today was great. Thank you for allowing me to be a part of it."

"You don't have to thank me for that. I'm just happy you could be here. How are you?"

"To be honest, I've never been better."

"How are things with you and Mark?"

"Over for good," I state. "When he realized Haley would get most of his assets, he moved to some part of Wisconsin with her, over a month ago and I haven't heard from him."

"Do you think he'll really let you go?"

"I don't know but I'm celebrating the small victories, as they come."

"Speaking of victories. Did you see the conclusion of David's trial? It has been streamed live on Channel 4, all week." I ask him. "He recanted his guilty plea at the urging of his attorneys because they thought he'd get off."

"No, I couldn't bring myself to watch it but I did see the breaking news of him being found guilty. I knew he'd turn on Jimmy and Mark, Sr. because he's a coward. Finding out Jimmy was dead was a relief to me. Does that make me a bad person?"

"No, you didn't kill him. Besides, he being dead is one less molester parents have to worry about and I don't feel bad about saying it. Mark's dad, on the other hand, I'm glad he and David are being made to pay for their sins. The saddest part of this, they have no remorse. They are making themselves out to be the victims when they are the ones who started all this." She replies.

"They are cowards and I only wish this had happened years ago. Gwen, they have been breaking young men, for years and going on about their lives. They stood in pulpits and on the grand stages lying about loving God, then going to molest the very boys they were sent to protect. They were living in the fancy houses while we were left to live in the darkness of our brokenness. How could they even look at themselves in the mirror?" I take a breath when she touches my arm. "I'm sorry, this stills riles me up but I'm working through it in therapy."

"I can only imagine."

"I went to my mother's grave," I announce, changing the subject.

"You did? When?"

"Yesterday, before I came here. I found out she was buried next to my brother and there was some things I needed to get off my chest. In the end, I forgave her because I could no longer hold her accountable, for what she allowed. I only wished I'd had the courage to tell her to her face. I wanted her to know how bad I was broken."

"I believe she knew because there is no way, you can serve a God like the one we serve and He not hold you accountable. Bible shares in Proverbs thirteen and thirteen, *'the one who despises the word will be in debt to it, but the one who fears the commandment will be rewarded.'* She knew, I know she did and she paid for it."

"Look at us getting healed," I say smiling. "I'm proud of us."

"So am I but I have a question. Are you ready to sign these papers?" She asks reaching for an envelope on the table.

"Yes, I am."

She spreads the papers out and I begin to flip through them.

"You have read over these, right?" She inquires. "I don't need you talking about, Gwen took my stuff, when all this is over."

"Hush woman. Yes, I've read every page and I am good with everything."

"Great, then let's do this." She hands me a pen and after a few minutes, we're done signing, including the papers for my paternal rights to be severed.

"It is finished," she says, trying to sound cheerful but her voice cracks. I pull her into me. "I'm sorry, I didn't think I would cry but it feels like a part of me is dying."

The baby cries, she sits up and wipes her face. I kiss her on the cheek. "I'm going to let you go."

"You don't have to rush."

"I have a late flight tonight because I have to work in the morning and I don't want to keep you and the baby up."

"You don't have to run each time you come home, you know? Whatever bad memories that once welcomed you, in this city, are destroyed and can be replaced with new ones."

"I know and I believe that but I really have to get back." I stand and pull her into a hug. "Thank you for everything."

"Boy, stop thanking me," she says hitting my arm. "No matter how we ended, I still believe in how we started and for that, I take nothing. You didn't keep your promise—"

"Ah man, I thought you forgave me?"

"I do and although you didn't keep your promise; your healing makes up for it. Stay on the right road, find love again, be you and be free."

"I pray the same for you."

She hugs me tight before I grab my things and walk out. When I get to my truck, I release the tears I'd been holding. "God, I thank you for not allowing me to destroy what you created. Cover Gwen and Jason, forever and amen."

Gwen

I watch Jacque walk out and I release the remaining of the tears.

"God, I thank you for restoration and healing. Thank you for allowing me to not destroy what you've created. Cover Jacque so that he becomes who you've destined him to become. Protect him and keep him safe, on his journey. Amen."

Just a word

Thank you for taking the time to read Broken. I pray this book has helped you, in some way. For me, this book pulled from places I didn't know existed because I've been this broken girl. Although I've never been abused, I have been broken and not able to love myself, enough, because of an absentee father. It didn't matter that I had a grandfather, uncles and even a step dad and daddy-in-love who was there; a piece of me was still broken.

One day, I wrote a letter to the father whose DNA runs through my veins and last name typed on my birth certificate. The father who lives within the confines of the same city and the father who has made other children, them he abandoned too. In this letter (I sent to him via Facebook Messenger), I told him I forgave him.

See, truth is, he was the one missing out but I was the one messing up. He was the one who'd abandoned us but I was the one angry. He was the one who walked out and I was the one, allowing folk to walk all over me. I had to stop it! He couldn't do it because, he didn't care so I released myself by forgiving him and vowing to never be this broken girl again.

I want the same for you.

This is why I'm sharing a part of the book again which I penned in a devotional, titled 'This is your pardon.' I need you to read it carefully because your freedom depends on you coming out of what you've sentenced yourself too.

This is your pardon …

When you've been in prison for a while, after being found guilty, the governor has the ability to grant you a pardon. Now, the pardon doesn't remove the offense from your record but you can no longer be held to the restrictions of your previous charge. In other words, a pardon forgives you for the crime you committed, either because you were wrongly convicted or the punishment you've received was too harsh for the crime.

As people of God, we will make mistakes, we will go through some things and we will have things happen to us that we can't control. When things happen, as they will; we tend to carry the weight with us, from place to place and relationship to relationship. A person who has been abused, carries that abuse. A person who has been broken, will carry the brokenness. A person who has been hurt will carry the hurt. The sad reality, it'll show up every time you think you're doing okay.

Why? Because you've sentenced yourself to a lifetime of recycling instead of destroying. Beloved, it's time you go free. You've spent too much time making yourself pay for a mistake you made. You've spent too much time in darkness, ashamed of what you've done. You've allowed people the power to continually make you pay for something they claimed to have forgiven you for. Today, this is your pardon. You shall no longer be ashamed, hold your head up. You shall no longer sit in the dark, replaying what happened to you, come out and be free.

Romans 8:1-3 says, *"So now there is no condemnation for those who belong to Christ Jesus. And because you belong to him, the power of the life-giving Spirit has freed you from the power of sin that leads to death. The Law of Moses was unable to save us because of the weakness of our sinful nature. So God did what the law could not do. He sent his own Son in a body like the bodies we sinners have. And in that body God declared an end to sin's control over us by giving his Son as a sacrifice for our sins."*

Baby, consider this your pardon. You are free and the chains are no longer holding you. Take up your mat and walk. Go, your faith has made you whole. This is your pardon. Oh, if you find yourself still stuck, it's because the only person that can hold you back, once God releases you, is you.

You are pardoned.

You are free.

About the Author

Lakisha Johnson, native Memphian and author of over fifteen titles was born to write. She'll tell you, "Writing didn't find me, it's was engraved in my spirit during creation." Along with being an author, she is an ordained minister, co-pastor, wife, mother and the product of a large family.

She is an avid blogger at kishasdailydevotional.com and social media poster where she utilizes her gifts to encourage others to tap into their God given talents. She won't claim to be the best at what she does nor does she have all the answers, she is simply grateful to be used by God.

Again, I thank you for taking the time to read my work! I cannot express what it means to me every time you support me! If this is your first time reading my work, please check out the many other books available by visiting my Amazon Page (search Lakisha Johnson).

For upcoming contests and give-a-ways, I invite you to like my Facebook page, AuthorLakisha, follow my blog https://authorlakishajohnson.com/ or join my reading group Twins Write 2.

Or you can connect with me on Social Media.

Twitter: _kishajohnson | Instagram: kishajohnson | Snapchat: Authorlakisha

Email: authorlakisha@gmail.com

Also available

The Family that Lies: Forsaken by Grayce, Saved by Merci

Born only months apart, Merci and Grayce Alexander were as close as sisters could get. With a father who thought the world of them, life was good. Until one day everything changed.

While Grayce got love and attention, Merci got all the hell, forcing her to leave home. She never looks back, putting the past behind her until … her sister shows up over a decade later begging for help, bringing all of the forgotten past with her. Merci wasn't the least bit prepared for what was about to happen next.

Merci realizes, she's been a part of something much bigger than she'd ever imagined. Yea, every family has their secrets, hidden truths and ties but Merci had no idea she'd been born into the family that lies.

https://www.amazon.com/dp/B01MAZD49X

The Pastor's Admin

DISCLAIMER This is Christian FICTION which includes some sex scenes and language.

Daphne 'Dee' Gary used to love being an admin … until Joseph Thornton. She has been his administrative assistant for ten years and each year, she has to decide whether it will be his secrets or her sanity.

And the choice is beginning to take a toil.

Joseph is the founder and pastor of Assembly of God Christian Center and he is, hell, there are so many words Daphne can use to describe him but none are good. He does things without thinking of the consequence because he knows Dee will be there to bail him out. Truth is, she has too because … it's her job, right? A job she has been questioning lately.

Daphne knows life can be hard and flesh will sometimes win but when she has to choose between HIS SECRETS or HER SANITY, this time, will she remain The Pastor's Admin?

https://www.amazon.com/dp/B07B9V4981

Dear God: Hear my Prayer

Since the age of 14, Jayme's life has been hell and she has one person to thank for it, Pastor James Madison.

He stood in the pulpit on Sundays waving the same hands that abused her at night. He glorified God with the same mouth he used to chip away her self-esteem, daily. He was a man of God who had turned her away from the same God he told people they needed to serve.

He was the man who was supposed to pray for, take care of and eventually love her. Instead he preyed on, took advantage of and shattered her heart before it had a chance to truly love someone else.

Now, 14 years and a son later, she finds herself needing God yet she doesn't know how to reach Him. She longs for God but isn't sure He can hear a sinner's prayer until she starts to say, Dear God.

https://www.amazon.com/dp/B079G68BN3

The Marriage Bed

Lynn and Jerome Watson have been together since meeting in the halls of Booker T. Washington High School, in 1993. Twenty-five years, a house, business and three children later they are on the heels of their 18th wedding anniversary and Lynn's 40th birthday. Her only request ... a night of fun, at home, with her husband and maybe a few toys.

Lynn thinks their marriage bed is suffering and wants to spice it up. Jerome, on the other hand, thinks Lynn is overreacting. His thoughts, if it ain't broke, don't break it trying to fix it. Then something happens that shakes up the Watson household and secrets are revealed but the biggest secret, Jerome has and his lips are sealed.

Bible says in Hebrews 13:4, "Let marriage be held in honor among all, and let the marriage bed be undefiled, for God will judge the sexually immoral and adulterous." But what happens when life starts throwing daggers, lies, turns and twists?

https://www.amazon.com/dp/B07H51VS45

Still Fighting: My sister's fight with Trigeminal Neuralgia

What would you do if you woke up one morning with pain doctors couldn't diagnose, medicine couldn't minimize, sleep couldn't stop and kept getting worse?

What would you do if this pain took everything from your ability to eat, sleep, wash your face, brush your teeth, feel the wind, enjoy the outdoors or even work? What would you do if this pain even tried to take your life but couldn't shake your faith?

Still Fighting is an inside look into my sister's continued fight with Trigeminal Neuralgia, a condition known as the Suicide Disease because of the lives it has taken. In this book, I take you on a journey of recognition, route and restoration from my point of view; a sister who would stop at nothing to help her twin sister/best friend fight to live.

It is my prayer you will be blessed by my sister's will to fight and survive.

https://www.amazon.com/dp/B07MJHF6NL

Other Available Titles

2:32AM: Losing Faith in God

The Forgotten Wife

Chased

The Family that Lies: Merci Restored

Bible Chicks: Book 2

Doses of Devotion

You Only Live Once: Youth Devotional

HERoine Addict – Women's Journal

Be A Fighter – Journal

These can be found on amazon or www.authorlakishajohnson.com

Made in the USA
Middletown, DE
01 July 2019